The Runaway

By Angel Simpson

To Longer
With love

ISBN 978-1-326-55773-7

Please contact the author by email at simpson-v1@sky.com

Dedication & Acknowledgements

I would like to dedicate this book to all those who are going through and do not know how to get through. The darkness will always seem more prominent than the light, so whether you are male or female, I hope my book inspires you and helps you through your darkest hours. You will see break throughs God is watching over you and you can do this.

I would like to thank God for all that He has brought me through. Heather for always inspiring me and Dominic, my son, who kept me sane when I thought the book was getting too hard to cope with. My son Marseille, for pushing me to finalise my book by asking me to have a draft ready for his birthday and my daughter Mareshah for giving total encouragement in getting on with my writing. A big thank you goes out to my partner who allowed me to express my thoughts and ideas with him and pushed me into doing better in my life, more than I ever thought I could. Dorothy, Donut, I know I can never bring you back, but I will never forget you either; this is also for you.

I love you all so much. Some of the songs in this book are mine and some are not but if you recognise some of them feel free to singalong, relax and receive whatever it is you need to receive from it.

Blessings to all
Angel

Contents

00: Introduction

Finally...
She got fed up with waiting
For her knight in shining armour to
Rescue her
So, she got up
She got dressed up and
She climbed out of the tower and
Rescued herself... TBC...

True love is not perfect. It rises, and it falls. It laughs, and it bawls. It bears no ill but carries all. In its perfect imperfection, it can make you laugh and make you cry, bring out laughter or a sigh, kiss hello or wave bye, bye, never mind the lows and highs. If it is yours don't hold too tight, just let it fly both day and night. But on the other hand, I say, don't hold too loosely or it will stray. Love is the richest gift a person can give but some don't know how to give it to you. This should not stop you however from learning how to give it to yourself. Find yourself a role model. Find yourself a friend. Find yourself a lover but most of all FIND YOURSELF...

Whatever you have been through, changing or creating little things will not change where you are going, and whether you like it or not, it will help you to find you... You have tried to fit in, and it has not worked. So now let me ask you a question. "Why would you want to fit in when you were born to stand out...?" I dare you to be that person...

We are all misfits in this world and until we accept this fact, we will keep searching for an ideal that is not real. Some may have been rejected at birth with no parents. Some during life due to unforeseen circumstances and some may have faced heartache with astronomical pain; whatever the situation, you can get through this. You can get over this and you can build a future for yourself, but you have to do this for yourself because everybody is busy facing their own situations, pains, fears and insecurities. There will be times when you have to stop; this does not mean you have to stop living, it just means that at times you will need to pause, take a deep breath and tell yourself 'I can do this,' 'I can get over this,' 'I am worth loving for me,' 'I don't have to be special to anyone else as long as I know who I am' and 'if the only person who loves me is God, then that is enough for me.'

01: Everyday In Captivity

Every day for as long as she could remember, she had sat in the attic looking through the bars, hatching her escape plan; she had seen most of the house, the bits he allowed her to, and she knew how to do it just not when and that was the most hurtful part of it all. She had tried many times before, but he had caught her and each time he did, it became harder to escape.

He became more vigilant, and she grew wearier; like let's see how far you can get today and then as if deliberately he would step to one side and leave the door ajar. She wasn't foolish though. She knew he was there hiding somewhere, waiting to pounce and drag her back into her tiny shell. That, however, was not the worse part of it all. The worse part of it was that he seemed to enjoy her attempts so that he could relish his nonstop fury upon her and each time it would be more severe than the last until... She simply seemed to give up and now the door would be left open for longer. She would just simply gaze at it and wonder but she would not even as much peak her head round to see if the coast were clear. *{NO NOT EVER – NEVER DARE AND REMEMBER, YOU BETTER BEWARE}*.

Had he finally broken her enough or had he just tamed her barely enough. He wasn't sure but he was certain inside himself that he was either all the way or at most ninety percent of the way.

Every day he would lay her food at the door and ask her a question and if she got it right, she ate and if not, she starved.

Sometimes, as if to appease his guilty conscience, he would offer her a joke – For instance, "Would you like a slice of 3.14" he would ask, and she would politely reply "Yes please" and laugh as loud as she could to let him know she found this joke particularly funny. She had heard all his jokes more than a hundred times but she knew not to laugh meant punishment so she laughed and was fed her 3.14 and to those of you who do not understand it is pie or should I say pye as it is properly spelt.

She had sometimes wondered why she hadn't died by now and at other times she wondered how she had survived for so long, but she also wondered how much longer before her body would give up from the abuse and her soul would leave this lonely planet, this lonely country, this lonely town, this lonely house, and most of all, this lonely room. The only thing to keep her mind active were the songs she sang and because she still had the privilege of having a CD player which she could play CDs he had lost interest in, not before though and if he felt she was getting too much enjoyment from them then he would take them back. He would even break some if he felt she was stepping too much out of line just to see if she would/could be bothered to cry.

He had no friends and if he died then she would die too of starvation as she felt sure nobody knew she was there. Well at least this was her thinking as she saw no one come or go. He on the other hand would frequent the pub. When he did this, you could tell as he would return home and tell no one in particular that he loved them with all of his heart and eat to his heart's content. She would always smell the takeaway and imagine it was her eating it; she would even imagine it was her that was high on alcohol and would sing as low as she could so that he would not know she was awake. If he had a mind to know then she would have something coming to her because in his twisted mind it was his to take. She was in his house so his rules, his law and his vengeance was what she lived by. She turned off the CD player and snuck into bed as quietly as she could. Any sound and he would be up there as faster, or faster, than the speed of sound, ripping at her clothes and demanding her to give in to his needs, his desires and his wishes. She could not say no as this would lead to a beating.

She was surprised that the neighbour's weren't suspicious and didn't wonder why they could hear wailing coming from the house. Was it because the walls were thick, were they deaf or out at work all the time? Were they like him and were they drunk all the time or was it because they chose not to hear her cries for help, chose not to hear the banging on the walls on his sober and gone out to work days. She had no clue which one it was, but it had to be one of the above and she decided to discount the fact that they chose to ignore because that would be heartless.

Then one day it happened. *{NO NOT EVER – NEVER DARE AND REMEMBER, YOU BETTER BEWARE}* He had been so drunk the night before that when he left her room, he left the key in the door. Her heart pounded in her mouth. He had never ever done that before. Was he letting her go? Yeah right! She looked around the room for a moment and thought leave the key there. It's another test and he wants what he wants and he might end up killing her this time. She grabbed the key and locked herself in and thought about pushing the key under the door. This way she would have passed the test and maybe he would leave her alone but no not that. As he left the house and banged the door shut, she thought she

9

could hear him outside the door. It's a test, it is a test. He's waiting for me and that will be my chance gone forever. She lay down and slept for a while and thought some more. What if he came back and found the key missing? He might change the lock or even leave her in there to supposedly starve.

She drew a deep breath and unlocked the door. She peeked her head round the door, nothing, and so without a second thought she went for it. She ran down the stairs feeling as though she hadn't touched any of them and burst out through the front door into freedom. It was then she realised she hadn't thought this through and that she was not dressed. She had no shoes and no coat on. It was so cold compared to inside which was like a furnace.

The sun hit her unwashed face and the sound of the traffic and people were confusing, but she had to go. What time was it and what direction would he be coming back from. She had to go but where and how but still she had to go and go fast. She had been tiny but now she was long and dangly, and her legs felt weak, but she urged them to move to somewhere, anywhere. She felt that she was not just freeing herself but all of those in her situation. If there was such a thing! She ran for all women and children and baby girls. She ran for all her life – she ran. Suddenly a hand grabbed at her and she will never know if it were him or a stranger but the sound of her deafening scream, a scream that could have deafened everyone within a ten mile circumference, the hand let go and she took off again and ran. Nobody needs or wants to draw attention to themselves and so she felt more confident the further away she got. Still she could not slow down just in case *{NO NOT EVER – NEVER DARE AND REMEMBER, YOU*

BETTER BEWARE} they were the words swimming around in her mind.

She didn't remember much of the world and it was now foreboding and gloomy and she began to feel like a patient who had escaped from some mental asylum. She knew about this because he had mentioned this to her before *{NO NOT EVER – NEVER DARE AND REMEMBER, YOU BETTER BEWARE}*. Oh God no more, please shut up and leave me alone, get out of my head and stop talking to me.

Now where could she go – who was there that she remembered that she could talk to or was this the moment to start a new life and was this even possible given the fact that he might find her and take her back to where she didn't want to be anymore. Food, how would she eat now and sleep – where...? She had to get away and far away from here but where was here. Becoming someone new would not be hard as she didn't really know who she was to begin with. A name, I am going to need a name.

BY VALERIE SIMPSON

02: My Name Is...

A name is not an easy thing to choose especially when you have never had one and I, now that I am and I, had to think quickly. First however, I needed to look around and find myself and where I was. This city, and I do think it is a city, is so big and I could never have imagined that given the fact that I have now gone from one room being my whole world to being out in the real world.

It is BIGGGGGGGG. I saw...
People begging money and
People begging food,
People that were sat there
Looking all in a mood
I saw people running to and fro and
People with nowhere to go,
I saw the up and the down,
The smile and the frown.
They cried and they laughed,
Went slow and went fast.
There was one thing they had in common,
They didn't see me.

I sat near a group of people having their lunch, but I knew not to look too hungry as that would have gotten me scolded in my room and then the beatings would have started, instead I looked at the sky which was bigger than the square and no bars to obstruct the full view. It's funny what you take for granted isn't it, even in captivity you get fed, not all the time but you know what I mean. Animals are caged and now looking at these people who were supposed to be free; even they looked as though they had their own restraints on them. They looked the same in the same type of clothes; they sounded the same and even complaining about the same things to each other. They were saying things like, "I totally agree with you," and "Did you hear what she said today in the office, my word that should have been a disciplinary." "You are so right." How can you be so right when you don't know anything about anything, just saying I guess...?

It has been a long day for me now and I feel so tired; even though I didn't like it at least I had a roof over my head and a bed to sleep in at night and now I remember again that I have no shoes and no coat. Could you have not been more stupid that all you have is this stupid piece of paper that you grabbed; oh, heck should I just try to go back now because I have no clue of where to go from here. Double heck, I don't even know where I came from. Where did I live and now where am I to go now the only true fact that I do know is, I had better find somewhere and fast or I will die from the cold; not so much hunger because I know hunger and I can deal with that.

I have had people throwing paper at me and thank God for the fact that I do remember what money looks like – he showed me some – and I heard about it I think before being in that room. Time to get up and go again before the rain comes. Try something or die from trying nothing the choice is quite simple.

"Hi, I need a room" I say as I enter a large motel, hotel holiday inn – sorry I did say I liked songs. It's a hostel and he looks real nice and yes everyone would give where I have just come from. He barely looks up "Name?" "What?" "I said, **NAME**" **"My NAME IS... ALEXAND, ALEXANDRA... XAVIER**. Yes Alexandra Xavier." "£45.00 per night, Money?" "I have none but this." I had nothing much on me but my two hands and I was hoping he would take me in, but he was kind enough to show me the door without swearing – too much. I had no money really, no room and no clothes but at least I had a name and that was a good start.

The streets get harsh at night and when you have nowhere to go it seems even harsher and I know this even more now. Why do I dream of him and his home? Why should I want to go back to what I hated before? *{NO NOT EVER – NEVER DARE AND REMEMBER, YOU BETTER BEWARE}*. Oh God when will those words ever leave me alone. I don't know what he did to my mind, but I do know I don't like it not one little bit. SHUT UP!!!!!!!!! FFS – I also heard him say that once and I guess I am saying it the right way.

Sleep – hard to do when you really are hungry, and I have never been this hungry – ever. Walk, walk, walk, and maybe the mind will be too tired to think of food and shelter. They say that things are supposed to get easier the older that you get and man I wish it were true. I am supposed to be having the time of my life but that doesn't seem to have come true, well not so far. I had a home and now I don't. I had food and once again none now. I had a bed and now... stop talking Alexandra. I like that name – I think it's so me or maybe not – I can imagine Alexandra being beautiful with long flowing hair – oh God why didn't I bring my comb or toothbrush. I must smell now. Sleep now – how hard can that be – harder than I thought.

"Follow me" a voice says from nowhere and being as I have nothing to lose, I obey. The voice leads me to a charity shop where they have left some things outside and I am guessing it is for the shop when it opens but now, I don't care as it seems to have nearly everything I need. A dress, yes, it's too big but who cares and at last shoes. A coat – now I have a red dress, a green coat and purple shoes. Does it sound terrible well guess what, it looks far worse. The one good thing is they don't smell. I stuff the paper in my brand new second hand pocket. The voice is now telling me to run and so I run – I don't know where but it guides me along the way. This way, come on, faster it says and at last it says over here. Shelter wow this is soooooo gooooood. Now to sleep and the voice must be thinking the same as it stops talking or should I say shouting. To sleep – this is beginning to feel so lonely and I never had a thought for how that would be. In the house I was lonely but at least I had him. *{NO NOT EVER – NEVER DARE AND REMEMBER, YOU BETTER BEWARE}*. Scratch that he had me and now we most probably have no – one.

I know he is hard to get out of my head and as bad as he treated me at least it was better than what I have now. Silence, I hate it, now the thoughts in my head will not shut up and it is driving me crazy, why am I nostalgic for something that was not good for me, why do I feel like crying. Oh God the voice is back and the sun is shining again. I must have fallen asleep and now my body aches – moving is hard now and I really want to run back but no, I won't do that, and even if I could, I shouldn't.

Right up and now the voice is telling me to eat and I am willing. I should look at the voice, but I'm scared it could be him taunting me before taking me back. One, two, three and here goes. Oh he's not old and not very smart unlike him on good days with his suit and tie. He is short and quite young I think even though he looks worn and weary. Thank you I say as the voice hands me some bread. The voice tells a joke and I laugh, I laugh so loud I scare the voice and so I shut up. Note to self – no need to laugh so loud he will not beat me.

When will things change and when will I become me for once. The voice is looking at me like he's confused or something, so I bow my head and eat and I don't look up again until I am finished. The voice stretches a hand to me, and I slap the hand. Oh, shit the voice was just giving me more food. "I'm sorry," I yell as fast as I can and the voice moves back even faster. After that, the voice just throws food in my direction like I were some kind of animal not to be gotten too close to and that suits me just fine. After all when he got too close it was because he wanted what he wanted. Once upon a time all I had was him and now I have the voice and I don't even know for how long. What if I fall asleep and the voice leaves me like I left him? Life is so full of questions and one day I will get some answers.

Who was I before yesterday, who am I today and who will I be tomorrow? I know that I have a whole lifetime to work that out but how long will my life be. It could end tonight and then I would never know – one step at a time – one day at a time.

When the voice speaks it never shuts up and then now more food throwing. I'd laugh if it were not so stupid but at least I have food. I would move on but for now the voice is all I have for now and at least the voice doesn't want anything from me in return, at least for now should I say. I guess at some point I should help and get food too. Okay here goes, just throw yourself into this thing and go for it. What do you have to lose?

A lost McDonalds, well she shouldn't have turned her back on it for that long. Market guy has given me apples – well thrown apples at me to get me to leave. Some bread for the birds and now for me. Not bad, not bad at all – the voice should be happy with my efforts. Oh no where is he, please God say he hasn't gone, not now, not yet – please come back. I wait all day, but the voice has gone and is not coming back for me.

I move on – this is the first time I have genuinely cried for someone and I don't even know why yet I cry all the same. My McDonalds is eaten in silence and now I feel the cold again. It's not really cold but it is empty. I'll leave an apple just in case the voice returns and this way he will know I tried to find him. Time to move on...

03: A Purpose For Everything

For every heart
That finds a love,
There is a heart that cries.
For every dream
That is reborn,
There is a dream that dies.
For every day
That's filled with sun,
There is a day of rain.
For every hour
Of joy we fill,
There is an hour of pain.
For every smile
Upon one's face,
There is a tear to cry.
For every fond
Hello we say,
There is a sad goodbye,
For every new face
In this world
There is a grave to see,
For every heart
That's open wide,
There's one without a key.

BY DOROTHY WYNTER

04: A Brand New Day

Well, here we go into a brand-new day and a brand new adventure. You have to see things this way or you will despair. I hear voices all around me, but none sound like him or the voice and now I miss both but nothing, no nothing, is forever and I am learning this faster and faster. I look around as I walk mainly because I cannot afford to go round in circles and delay progress. It takes forever but now I see fields and some cows, chickens and some crazy cats playing in a field.

Cats Gone Wild

The cats have gone wild
Oh gosh they used to be mild
Hungry for food
And not in the mood
To conversate
And I can relate.

Hurry home baby
Hurry home to mum
She's got supper ready
And you will get some.

By ALMAC

Silly songs that go through my head and I let them as I walk. I realise now I can sing loud and nobody is there to stop me, so I sing, and I sing loud. *{No not ever – never dare and remember, you better..}.* NOT TODAY... You are not with me today so go away and leave me alone. Oh, crap I am alone.

The next few days were hard for me as I didn't trust to make a friend again. My only friend I think was the voice and he left without using his voice so now – no – no more friends who can come and go as they please. I work for food along this road, but nobody lets me in to bathe so I bathe in streams and rivers. I don't care who sees as I lost my shame a long time ago, not that anyone cares to know that and those who pass by look the other way.

They say that fat people are lazy. Well he used to anyway, that is not true, it is people with money who are lazy because they pay others to run around for them. I don't mind as they pay good, especially if you do well at what they want you to. I give them the fruits of my labour. Listen don't judge he used to take it for nothing so why not have somebody pay for it. I am now turning it into an art form and there is nothing wrong with that.

I now have enough money to get a coach somewhere, anywhere, and who knows, I may continue to go fruit picking as one man called it when I lay with him in the cherry field. So funny that; he plucked my cherry. Okay well not really but he didn't know that. When he had gone, I lay there still in the grass and closed my eyes with the sun beaming down on my face. It was blindingly good, no not that, and I would have stayed there all day had the farmer not told me, in not so nice words, to move on. I strolled with my head high and a biggish wad of money in my undies. Oh yeah time to change them.

I drifted into the small town and paid for a room – okay shed and made my bed to sleep. I was sure I could stay there for a while, but the owner kicked me out and although I wanted to fight, I didn't. My money he took it, not all but a lot. I carried on walking and now I felt better than I had done for years. Cherry trees, apple trees, ice cream and brain freeze.

Okay, here will do for the night and I bet it is him missing me now. I think about buying another coach ticket and I will have to let the coach people choose as I don't know where to go. "Alexandra Xavier," I say to myself. "You will go far with a name like that," I have to I reply and as if by magic I hear his voice but today I am determined to sing him out. Drown him in strong words.

Truth is I stole the name. Part was a story about a young woman who fell in love many times and to many men. She died. He let me have that book like a warning. The name Xavier, I saw on the table as I walked in and truth be told I didn't know how to say it but the guy behind the counter corrected me; must have thought I was just nervous but that was okay because I didn't want to tell him how many times I had wanted somebody to listen to me instead of me listening to them. I mean you can talk to the music, but it cannot reply and he did not listen; not once but now he doesn't have to because unlike some, I am free.

Every man has an equal right
To live and be FREE
No matter what colour, class or race he may be.

BY DENNIS BROWN

I am reminding myself of how much songs meant to me and singing them somehow releases and lot of tension. I lift my head to the sky and my hands to the Lord and thank Him for giving me music. Nobody knows unless you know what it is like to only see artificial daylight, dark nights with no dark knight to rescue you and only a stark bare room for company. Looking back, I do not know how I didn't completely go insane, but somebody out there must have loved me or just been on my side for me to be free and to be living the life I am now. This does remind me though that I need to wash and pretty soon, if not sooner, that period of time will be with me again and I need to be prepared for it when it happens. Nobody wants to help a tramp, but a smelly one is a no, no in this world.

I am now no longer as shy as I used to be, and I am now quite slick in what I have to do to survive and so with the little change I have I buy me some of the things I need, and I go to the food and clothes bank to find me some clothes. There are shops called the Cooperative that have clothes dumped on the floor that no one but no one wants anymore. If you are lucky you may find something that you like; it may not always fit but it has always been better than nothing. I can always collect a few pieces to keep me going for a while and dump them if they get too dirty. I am ashamed but did you know that you can walk into the swimming baths to use the toilet, sneak into the shower room and wash, change and even wash your smaller items before putting them under a hand dryer. Nobody asks any questions because they want to pretend they do not see you because if they see you they may have to help you and they don't want to so they pretend not to. I don't care anymore because it suits me just fine. Sometimes you can get lucky searching the lockers where people have forgotten to collect their pounds once they leave and at other times they are fake ones. Either way you make money by selling the fake ones for fifty pence a pop.

Instead of being angry shop owners who don't want you there, you keep their area clean. Once they see this, they let you stay a while. One place that I stayed for a while was owned by an Italian man and he used to pretend to throw food away, I mean good food, and I would take it. Out of gratitude I would make sure he always had a clean area. The more I cleaned the more food he left me until his manager fired him for helping me. I was broken for him, but he didn't mind as he told me "This is not my lot so I am free to be whatever I want to be" if that's the case it's alright.

Sometimes moving on was so easy but other times it was hard, and this was one of those hard times. He was a good man, and I will miss him, but his manager will regret it now as his yard was classified as one of the messiest places after and he almost was closed down – karma is so nice for some and he deserved it. I do smile when I think of that – a lot.

I didn't know about racism and so when I first heard the N word, I didn't know it was about me and to make it worse the person who said it was not even far off being my colour. I learn fast though and I stayed away from others who looked like him and sounded like him. The women were not so bad but I still chose not to trust just in case...

05: Live, Live, Live

I laugh when I feel like crying
I live though I feel like dying
I grin when the world is lying
I am water when the ground is drying

That's me for all the world to see
Living alone but living at ease
Living is a sting but living must be
What you make it to be bonded or free

You can fly like a bird up in the sky
Or sink like a rock by and by
You can soar on the air way up high
Or plummet down and probably die

The choice is yours but at all times choose life
Because if you don't it will cut like a knife
And one day you'll find that you want to live
But death will take you so live, live, and give

VS - ALMAC

This is what I set out to do and this is what I was going to do from this day on. These are the words that I decided I would tell myself and it would be my motto. Live, live, live, and when I could find a pen, pencil or some writing implement – I would write those words and leave them behind for someone, anyone who might need them or be reminded to live. Death is not an option, and neither is failing so go on and on and on and on... Keep pushing because pushing is all you can do when you feel like quitting, giving up or not to fight anymore.

06: The Journey – The Song – The Singer

We are all on a journey in this life, some days are up and
other days are down and that is the
Way it is for the most of us.

You have the good and the bad
The happy and the sad
Times when you want to sing
Times when you want to sink

There are days when nothing
And no one gives a fling
But you can make it because
In life you can be anything

You can't lie down
And you can't roll over
Because in this world
Ain't no one gonna love ya

Truth be told
In life you gotta run
And when you look around you
Ain't no one having fun

Make the money, get the honey
Drive the car and make it big
But if you lose it all don't look for me
I'll be elsewhere doing my thing
Laugh at me if you want to
Hate me also if you must

But when you're busy losing
I'll be kicking up some dust

07: A Place To Call My Own

Imagine, even after all that had happened, I yes, I found somewhere to sleep and eat. It was good for the first time. The room was dark and smelled like pee but I didn't care. It was off the streets and it was cold but lovely. I began for the first time ever not regretting leaving him behind. **{NO NOT EVER – NEVER DARE AND REMEMBER, YOU BETTER...}** I shook those words off as fast as they came to my mind and for the first time it was like an open wound that had started to heal.

One of the others in this place had some bleach and a brush, the things I needed, and so in exchange I cleaned for her and she gave me some of what I needed. She didn't give me all as she figured giving me all would mean I would stop helping her and man she needed me. I cleaned and she was grateful. We even stole together and when we did, we took it in turns to look out for each other. I asked for a name and she gave me the name Sushanna. I didn't know if it was her real name but quite frankly, I didn't give a damn. We had food and that was all we wanted for the moment.

Sushanna had run away from home as she wanted to live her life her way. She didn't want to be told, or so she told me, what to do. She was going to make it big no matter what her parents said – yeah right – living here was making it big huh. She was from a country where they told you how to live and who to marry. She was not into that kind of crap and I could relate to her.

Tall, slim and beautiful with long black flowing hair and with eyes as dark as midnight she could have been a model, I think.

27

She was not like me really; I am shorter with eyes like a cat and so I gained the name 'Puss' and sometimes 'Kitten' because they saw me as a bit naive. Anyway...

I laid out the tiny things that I had gathered and thought, let's make the most of this. The room was alright, after all it wasn't ever going to be a palace but whatever you think a place is then that is what it will be. I walked the streets, remembering not to forget my steps, and looked for things to make my room, my new home, and my new dwelling place as homely as possible. Lamps that were thrown out and old quilts were all good things. I dared not leave anything too long as it might not have been there when I got back. I found an old chair and man many times I wanted to throw it; the damn, sorry darn, thing was fricking heavy. I made it back though and when I did, I was so proud.

Books were brilliant because they made me look so edumacated. An old rug, a lamp – it didn't work but so what – a table one of the girls didn't want and an old television. For the first time a television. I couldn't wait to switch this thing on but when I did it blew up – now I know why they didn't want it. Another television found and this time I turned it on with caution. It worked and now I was set not though for this lonely planet, this lonely country, this lonely town, this lonely house, and most of all, this lonely room at times.

Sleeping though was not an issue for me as I could lock and open my door. What made some laugh though was me locking and unlocking my door. I did this from time to time to remind myself that I could, but somebody told me NEVER to leave my room unlocked and always to leave the key in the door to let others know it was my domain.

It was on one of my little jaunts when I met him, or should I say he, as usual, found me. Fernando was singing on the corner and the words of the song jumped at me like stop and listen to me.

I was born by the river in a little tent
Oh and just like the river I've been running ev'r since
It's been a long time, a long time coming
But I know a change gonna come, oh yes it will

{It has to change}

It's been too hard living, but I'm afraid to die {wow}
Cause I don't know what's up there, beyond the sky
It's been a long, a long time coming
But I know a change gonna come, oh yes it will
I go to the movie and I go downtown
Somebody keep tellin' me don't hang around
It's been a long, a long time coming
But I know a change gonna come, oh yes it will
Then I go to my brother
And I say brother help me please
But he winds up knockin' me
Back down on my knees, oh
There have been times that I thought I couldn't last for long
But now I think I'm able to carry on

{Sam Cooke} I knew the song as soon as he started to sing it; I had heard it but tonight it resonated in my soul. It took me so much to a place in my dreams, nightmares, and thoughts that without even thinking I grabbed his mic and sang for all my heart.

Oh, you should have seen his face, he hated me, and I could feel it, but I couldn't stop. I sang for all my sorrows and for all my joys. I sang for yesterday, today, and tomorrow and I sang for hate and love. The money plunked into the hat and he still hated me but he didn't look at me anymore. More and more came and I had achieved another dream. Don't get me wrong I was not the most polished of singers, but my heart felt and lived every word that I sang and that was good enough for me and all who heard me. I was alive

It's been a long, a long time coming
But I know a change is gonna come, oh yes it will
It's been a long, a long time coming
But I know a change is gonna come, oh yes it will

So deep... so true... so honest... so spiritual... and so me...

I would go back to the same spot to look for him, but he would move around the town and I learned he had to do this to avoid the police. When I did find him, I would wait for him to ask me to sing but he didn't. I had never thought of myself as brave but when the music started and took over me, I took over the mic. The words would flow as though from another person's mouth, but it was me. He started to get used to me and I swear one day he even smiled. He would look for me after that and we became a couple – no, not like that – as singer and instrumentalist – instru – mental – list. Sounds like a crazy person who has a catalogue of things in their mind when you break it down into small chunks but that is what we were, and besides, I think I brought him more money. He had a younger person with him who would go around and collect change in a hat and look out for the police and other days I would suddenly start singing a song by the police whilst grabbing things to run.

Those were about the only days when I found I had a voice. Conversations were not me and so we, meaning I, just did a lot of silly smiling.

I never asked for money, just food and I never forgot to feed Sushanna when I got back. Sometimes I would find gifts at my door and I would open them like an overly excited child getting Christmas presents or that's what it looked and felt like in my mind's eye. I found my voice in singing but not in conversation – no that was going to take more time and so as if not to push neither Fernando the musician or Sushanna would rush me. They knew pushing me meant having me run and so they waited for me.

08: The Unspoken Grief – Words Left Unsaid

She had been so angry with her father and although he had been dead in her eyes for such a long time, his anger, pain, and abuse were still in her head, her heart and in her bones. When something hurts your heart, it can heal. When it torments your mind, you can find somebody to speak to, give you therapy and advise you of what to do next, but when it is in your bones it becomes deep seated, so rooted, so embedded that it is hard to separate it from the very core of your being.

She had walked the lonely corridors of life, living and becoming what she felt everyone had wanted from her, but deep down inside she had never lived a life of her own. She had lost herself somewhere along the line and despite searching, she could not find herself. She had liked what they liked, she had eaten what they ate, she had followed the directions that were given to her for her life; become a mother, she wanted to be, she had given up her name and now she was on the verge of giving up her life. This was the final chapter of her life and it felt good.

As she lay in her bed looking through the window of her life, she found peace, perfect peace and she knew it was the right time to lie down and sleep, endless sleep, peaceful sleep, quiet slumber sleep with no more pain and no more anger.

He had dealt the last blow of her life and the last blow to her heart and now her bones. It was bad at the time, but it was now fine because if it hadn't been him it would have been somebody else and she knew it was not going to leave until she was dead, full dead, no breath, no healing, no coming back, dead.

You die two ways:

01:     You can be alive physically, see the world going on around you full of life and be dead because you have no heart, no vision and no insight into anything going on around you. The walking dead is what I think they call it

02   You walk out of the will of God which is the very foundation of your life and become part of the walking dead; no soul, lifeless and hell bound.

Sorry three ways to die. You stop breathing...

I, she had made up her mind that she would never love and never give her heart to any man no matter how amazing he was and then she broke the rules.

01:     Never believe a word a man says
02:     Never trust in a man
03:     Never give anything to a man but take all you can
04:     Never let a man touch you

But then she met you...

09: Getting To Know Me – To Know You

Fernando had wanted to share my room but that was not on the cards – well not for now, I had to get to know his voice and to make sure Fernando didn't become him. I was not in the mood to become a prisoner in my new home at least not whilst I was finding my feet. Maybe the circumstances would change and I'd let him in the door.

Sleeping alone was no weird thing to me and even though my room was dark it was somehow a different kind of dark. Well at least I was free to turn on a light and stomp around – ish. Surviving was not easy but also not hard and I enjoyed watching my brand new second hand television. I enjoyed it so much that sometimes at night I had to remind myself to sleep. Singing was another joy and I started to even write song lists on old scraps of paper, only the ones that made my voice sound good and nothing too hard or in need of a lot of practice mind you.

I had my first fight over another lodger trying to take over my room and steal my gifts – first time for everything and until that moment I had not realised how territorial I could and would become. I took extra security measures before leaving my room after that, but it was worth it. This I guessed would be the first but not the last time for this kind of thing to happen. I know one day I will have to move on but for now I am fine doing what I am doing.

Memories are hard to get rid of but with time you can handle them and they do become less traumatic. Don't get me wrong, they don't disappear, but they do not hurt as much. Even in my dreams I could laugh at some of them. Yes, I did wonder if he was alive, but I also secretly wished him dead at other times. Now he would be the one to die alone with no one there to notice his passing. Please God I am sorry, but thoughts are thoughts and not deeds.

I need to get a job, but where with no fixed abode and at times begging can be hard. Stealing food and clothes from the tip can be hard, especially when you look through windows and see some eating foods that you wish you could have. The same things go into bins so you have no choice in what you eat. Oh well, to sell or not to sell and this is one of those days that I wish I had the courage to sell. *The Boxer – Simon & Garfunkel* comes to mind and so I sing it as loud as I can without upsetting Sushanna. She's been missing home, family and the happier times even though she can't go back – and there is no going back. I cannot compare going back with her and I cannot empathise as we have totally different reasons for not going back – returning – and remaining away from *the way we were*.

Okay tomorrow's play list:

The Boxer – Super
Memories – Excellent
Theme From Mash – Possibly
I Will Survive – Oh yes

I go in search of my musician and I don't find him and so upset, I think about going home but something says stay and sing, no music necessary as I am now getting a real good beat with an old tin bucket. It could almost pass for being a tin drum if you close your eyes and listen but it's not really a good substitute for Fernando. I think about quitting my search but at the same time I do not give up. Allie, I tell myself, you will find him and when you do you can both resume the patter you have together. I make some money but to be fair we need each other to make more – again to sell or not to sell – not yet. I'm not ready for that – **YET!!!** Just the thought makes me feel violently sick. What choice do you have if you don't sell? It's getting closer more and more and well I have to decide. I've made enough for a bottle of red wine and I am going to drink it and know how it feels to be high on high. I think you say it that way but who cares. Drink does not offer a solution, rather than that I feel it was money wasted, as I am sick all night and I don't know how he could have done this almost every night – no more.

Still searching and this has gone on for weeks, in between I sing and now dance. I've been watching some young girls dance and I mimic their moves, I'm getting better even though I'm not the best – moves are moves though and it seems to work at times more than others. People can be so heartless at times and I wonder why I continue to try but still I keep going with **THE HOPE** that one day the promise will happen going through my brain. I used to believe that I was Rapunzel, I heard the story somewhere, and a knight would charge my tower and rescue me. We would move into a palace and have children, love them and raise them happily. Now I realise that I have to rescue myself so I sell, and I am making more money than I ever dreamed I would. It is uncomfortable and I hate every moment of it – but money talks and bullshit walks. I have to hide the money under the floor boards in case somebody else finds it and I want to move into a home soon. I'll take Sushanna with me so she isn't left alone and lonely – **EVER**.

I ask questions but nobody seems to remember him, and nobody has seen him. Did my musician really exist or did I make him up. I couldn't have and I know he was there – he was – I say as though I am trying to convince myself. If it were a dream then it was recurring, recurring, recurring – just being a bit ironic. He must be somewhere, and I will find him because he is the other key in my ride to freedom. Now I think about the voice and how he is and I wonder if it's me that makes people just up and disappear without a trace. Now I panic and run home – Sushanna, Sushanna – no reply – has she gone too. *NO, NO, NO, NOOOOOOO*. "Keep it down would you, I'm sleeping." I hear Sushanna scream from her room and suddenly, even though she's angry, I am reassured that she is still there, and I am not totally alone.

I am physically and mentally tired now and feeling in need of rest. Not just for the body but also for the mind and soul. First, I check my hidey hole and put more money in; I eat in silence with no music or television. My mind is working overtime and I can't handle any more noise so I sit with the air as my company and watch the moon pine for the sun with the stars twinkle to lighten his mood. Okay *OTT* but it sounds so nice. I don't know how I have such an imagination, but I do and now – not right now – is the time to use it. So now tonight I rest and tomorrow I start again. To get up and to go out in search. I can't say why I feel this way, I don't have a clue, I just do and maybe somebody, someday and somehow will tell me. So, I will get up – *IF I CAN*...

10: Life Is Me...

In life you learn
When you crash and burn
That the friend you had
Will be the friend who'll leave

When the truth is out
And the hearts turn cold
It's there that you learn
That you've got to be bold

When the chips are down
And you're down and out
It's time that you must jump
And find a different route

Find another way to make
It through the day
Because you are the only one
Who can see things your way

And when the day is done
And you lay head down to sleep
Remember that you're number ONE
I can only rely on and that one – that is me

By VS – ALMAC...

11: Tomorrow's Dream – Last Night's Nightmare

I prayed, if praying is talking with God, and asked for a good night's sleep but instead it was a full blown nightmare.

I dreamt I was running through a long dark tunnel chasing a red balloon. It moved just out of my reach and as if to tease me and every so often it stopped. I would think, I'm gonna catch it and then it would move. It went so high that it looked as though it would be gone forever and then reappeared. I waited a while to make sure it had thought I had given up and then I pounced, it jumped and carried on moving. I ran and cried – I cried and I ran but I didn't get closer. I shouted at it, but it didn't stop. I held my hand out, but it didn't want to be held. I asked it for help, but it ignored my pleas and when I said I loved it – just like that – it exploded and fell dead on the ground. Was my love fatal...? I don't know, and it seems I don't know a lot of things, but there and then I vowed never to fall in love in case I killed it, or it killed me. Then I suddenly wake up with a start...

FUCK... I'm still here – how did that happen...?

I decide that today is the day to find a proper home and I go in search of my red balloon, sorry, I meant my new flat but I don't tell Sushanna because I want it to be a surprise.

I don't find it however, I do find Fernando, and suddenly the song has come back in my heart and the spring in my step is lighter than usual. I go to hug him but somehow he is colder than the day we met and I have a feeling it's me – no doubting that.

No, it's not me he says... I've been ill... didn't realise you missed me... I'm shocked that anyone cared enough... to miss me...

He talks a long time and I listen although all I really want to do is sing. I want to sing all the songs on my list, the ones I sang whilst I was waiting for Fernando to come back... I wanted to have the voice that he gave me, well I gave me through him. Why won't you let me sing...?

I fell ill... I had an operation... it hurt a lot... but It's over now... appendix... explosion... almost died... cried myself to sleep... but I am alive... made me think... what if I'm sick and nobody knows... what if I die and nobody cares...

Now at least I know so now can everything go back to how it was **YES... NO... MAYBE...**

Circle the one that is appropriate to the correct answer.

Now we no – longer speak but we do sing – so yes – is the answer. We do not need to speak because he knows I care and I know he needs me. We sing so long that the stars are out again and I think about my red balloon – will the dream happen again tonight. Cars are racing past us as we sit and eat in silence; no words spoken just our hearts beating in tune with the other. I want to laugh and say yes but I have to follow suit and remain silent so as not to break his chain of thought... I feel like I can read them, and I know they are happy. For once anyways.

I touch his hand and he jumps then puts it back telling me, without words, try again so I do and he does not move, does not look at me, does not try to hold my hand. I go to move my hand away and then resist the action for fear it may never again or that I would somehow lose the courage to do it again. So, I just sit... and pretend...

Now the contents of this day have to be positive for life to continue and I am determined to be this way just so that I can get somewhere.

Living is harder than I thought it would be and maybe that is why he was the way he was. To see things you dream of having but never possessing them. To live the lives of a dream but awaken in a nightmare. To want that distant star to come to you but the more you chase it the further away it gets from you. To see the gift but never be able to touch it and your goals to go unrealised to an unmarked grave.

A grave so full of all the things you should have had but were never able to get your hands on... Scratch that one that will never be me.

I stop saying that today is the day and just go for it and I walk into a hostel right off the street. I walk up to the counter and I tell the man behind the counter I am homeless and need somewhere to stay. I have money I say even though he is not listening – I have money – I repeat and then he looks at me. I wait for him to tell me to leave like this has happened before and then I notice his eyes soften and his face relaxes into a smile. He can tell that I really need to be there.

We go into his office and he fills out the forms for me. Alexandra Xavier... me Alexandra Xavier. I repeat it so that I can remember that is me. He asks me if I have clothes and I say yes, I will go collect them. He asks if I need to eat and I say no, then he lays food on the table and I demolish it faster than the government demolishing its country. I tried to stop myself and couldn't and he knew I would do that.

Afterwards he takes me to a room with a **BED** in it and a **SHOWER**. The bed has **CLEAN SHEETS – WOW** and **HEATING**. I got here on time as the weather is now getting colder. I want to shower but look at the bed, it is so inviting. "Come rest in me" it whispers, and I reply, "oh yes." After a good sleep I shower with **HOT WATER** – I mean real hot water and I feel alive again.

12: A Room Of My Own

When I get back to my room, I find that someone has tried to get in and Sushanna had driven them away. I collect my things and take Sushanna with me back to the hostel where she washes and I hear her sing – I have never heard her sing – she is terrible but it's good to hear her sing. Money safely hidden again, and we go to eat.

She loves me today not because she loves me but because she feels clean and satisfied for the first time in like forever. That night I sneak her into my room again and the feeling of having another body next to me as I sleep gives me comfort and warmth. I need that. She needs it too as she snuggles up close and closer to me. Her arms around me and her head leaning on me. We need each other, and we know it too well.

I get up early to go for breakfast {oh breakfast} she hides and I eat. I stash food for her to take back and the manager bids me a cheerful good morning. He smiles so nice and I wonder if he is looking to buy something from me like the other men who smile at me. He turns his head and throws a sandwich my way, "give this to your friend." Now I blush, I thought I was discreet now I know I wasn't. Then he breaks the silence and tells me "I am a Christian." "What...?" Christian...? "Like one of those people who hit you with a Bible" I ask. He, who I had left behind, had told me about people who went Bible bashing. Now I learned it was a figure of speech. Silly me that is not what it means at all. His name is Micah and he loves teaching the Bible and I love hearing him and his wife teach. His wife's name is Jonah. Apparently, her father had given her the name Jonah and instantly regretted it when she kept running away.

That made me laugh and it was then that I decided if I ever found a husband, I would like us to be like Micah and Jonah.

Whilst I did like doing the little bits of works that I do for Micah and Jonah I did miss the selling. It will never be the best thing for a girl to do, but it did give me contact, human contact, and money – lots of money. I had never had that kind of money before and when I sold I could buy anything I wanted and was never in need of begging.

I do listen to the preaching and I take it all to heart but as for telling me prostitution is wrong, to give it its rightful name, I'm not sure about that. Once when I sat in on their church thing, they taught about a woman caught in adultery and was about to be stoned. I thought in my head 'yeah don't try that crap on me,' but her Jesus stepped in and stopped it. I was so angry – all the men want you to give and not pay...? When it gets out it's always the woman's fault. Why not stone the man instead because she is just trying to survive. I think... as I remember that was one of the only times I got up and walked out.

Afterwards Micah tried to talk to me about it, but a man is not the one to talk to when it seems men do all the condemning of women and also the shaming. If he were to know I was a seller what would he say – would he kick me out...? Where would me and Sushanna stay then, and it would all be my fault – again. Anyways, all I hear is women should do not do this or that... Or what – we won't survive, we'll be killed, we will pay – oh shut up – it doesn't make sense. Maybe it's because I relate too many things to him and I am wrong, or they are, either way we will soon find out. I do love the singing though and they have a massive choir. They all dress in big black robes and they clap hands, jump and dance whilst they sing. They so have a lot of rhythm and I am thinking of going for that big style. They call themselves Pentecostal and I have to find out what that means and why they have chosen to use it as a title.

As much as some believe, I am simple, but I do love to learn – I do find kiddies books funny to – kinda like catching up on what it would have been like. Comedies and obviously musicals are on the list and even cartoons are good. For weeks I walked around telling everybody – I am groot – to all that they asked or told me. The looks on their faces was priceless and if I were heartless, I would have laughed openly only respect made me keep it inside.

It could be said that I have not seen enough of life to make a decision right now and it could also be said I have seen too much through his eyes but things will not always be the same and then we will know for certain which side of the fence that I am on. For now though we will take the days as they come.

Now he doesn't come to me for a talk, but his wife does. "Your friend will have to register for her own room" she says and even though Sushanna is too scared, I talk her into it, and she goes for it. Besides her room may no longer be there. She signs the forms but lies about her name. They know she's lying and guess she will tell the truth. Even though she has her room now she still sleeps in mine and cuddles closer to me more than a little child lost or having a nightmare. I do not move as when I do, she cries. I guess we are not that much different in that way, only I cry on the inside whereas I can see her tears she cannot see mine.

Proverbs 3:24 - When thou liest down, thou shalt not be afraid: yea, thou shalt lie down, and thy sleep shall be sweet.

She whispers the words for comfort, and I do believe they help, as soon as she whispers them, she sleeps and slumbers.

13: Life Goes On...

I know that things sound so good but as I am always on my feet, I have to think one step ahead and have a backup plan. I love it where I am, and it has been six months – yes six months in one place but soon I must move.

My dear Fernando is still around, and we sing to our hearts content. I then go back and hug Sushanna to sleep for her and me. In between I sell but I go as far as I can so that the Church folk don't see or find out about my sinful ways. I could lie and say that I need the funds but that is a lie. I want the funds and I am used to doing things my way. Right or wrong I do not want to depend on anyone.

I look at myself in the mirror from time to time and I reassure myself that it will all be worth it at the end and then I can stop being this person and go on with the new me and the new title I will give myself. A name can be changed, and a new one can be gained, especially when the one you have now is not even yours. It's all make belief and has to come to an end at some point. Why pretend. For now though I will live a life not a lie anymore.

Micah and Jonah are teaching us how to read better and getting us ready for college and I still wonder if he wants to buy. He still has given me no reason to feel that way, it's just a feeling I get and the way he looks at us when we are alone. I wonder if Jonah has any idea what I think and I wonder if she trusts him so much that she can go away and not doubt his faithfulness.

I believe that with this kind of teaching we will go far and we will have brighter futures to look forward to. I still have a problem with speaking my mind and this is not good. I have to find a way to overcome and be an "overcomer" as he, meaning Micah, says most Sundays.

I can relax now and I feel that life is getting better. My red balloon still appears and even though I don't want to, I still chase it. It always goes under the bridge and past the same park. It goes down a dark dingy lane and over a wall this time and that says a lot at times because anytime I think I have it trapped then it reveals it is the one that has fooled me. From now on I will not even bother; funny because you really can't control your dreams and how they play out. I do wonder if I will catch the red balloon or will it be joined by more heart wrenching, mind bending and heart breaking ones.

I get fed up of this and I look it up in a book of dreams only to find that I am chasing passion, love and my secret desires. Not catching it is me hoping and desiring so much and also being fearful. Now I can put it behind me I hope and move on with my life – *PLEASE*...

You know what, *TIME* to move on and no time to keep looking back. Ooh shopping time and I have the cash to do it. I've had to hide the money in several different places and most of it I keep on me as Sushanna is now watching me and I can see she is questioning the fact that I am in late and she has to sneak me in. She watches where I put things and I even believe she searches those areas. I even put rubbish there to see if she will comment on why I am hiding rubbish; you keep looking lady I am not telling you. If there was one good thing he taught me, it was how to hide the truth from others and how to hide your emotions – I'm not saying thank you mind you – I am saying good on you for those moments of antagonism, pain and hopelessness because that was my yesterday and never again my tomorrow.

I am free to be whatever I... whatever I want to be and it reminds me that the moment you give up on your hopes and dreams you may as well lie down and die and I am not ready for that; so with that I say goodnight and goodbye to all of the ones who hurt me abandoned me or lost belief in me; then I let it go like it were just wind blowing through the night skies.

For one of the only times as I remember it, I woke with a smile like a mile wide and it felt as though I had been wearing some ill fitting armour and had now taken it off. Priceless peace had filled the room and pain was gone forever, well at least for now; I had to use forever as I had to believe it wouldn't come back again.

Fernando on the other hand was going downhill quite fast and didn't seem to share my new found enthusiasm for life. He had been in hospital again and was not letting anybody see him at all. He couldn't keep me out and I fought him every step of the way and I won – we are the champions my friends...

I fed him and never let him know where the money came from. I gave him clothes and he never knew it was me. He became so delirious that he thought his family had found him and were once more looking after him and so I left him to believe it. He had to have something to hold on to and if it were this then so be it – AMEN.

We laughed so much in the days that followed and he told me

stories about his family. Fernando Antonio Graham was born on the 15th of July and spoke several languages; his family had high hopes for him and becoming a busker was not one of those hopes so when he did, they cut him off like a bad smell – sorry but true. He was the oldest and his brothers Simon, Kensal, Jimmy, Junior and Shaun had kept to the plan and done what was expected of them. His two sisters were the ones to stand by him and this infuriated the parents. Eventually Shauna and Simone were sent to live elsewhere so that he could not influence them anymore than he had. I thought of him as my hero after that. I had never done anything as herolc – all I had done is run away and hide from him, my past, and my bad memories.

14: Onwards And Upwards

As I arise from another day of sleeping, I give myself a chance to breathe in and out slowly and then get out of bed. For once I sleep alone and am glad to have some space for myself. Do you know how hard it is keeping somebody else together when you really don't know how to do the same for yourself...? I do and let me tell you it is no easy feat.

Breakfast for the first time tastes good and I wonder what I should do with myself for the day. I have not runaway or had a reason to runaway for a while now and it becomes a very disconcerting feeling. My stomach does not feel good today. In actual fact it hasn't felt good for a few weeks but I try not to focus on that. I am eating well, too well, and have now gained a bit of weight. I look at my rounding face in the mirror and I think of going on a die – yet.

I walk into town and look through the windows of the shops and I can see them staring back at me like, please move on, but I pretend not to see their glares and I continue to look through windows. I obviously do not shop as I have a lot invested in my mind. Buying a house some day would be good and having my own space to move about would be even better. No, I don't think I will have a room at the top of the house and if I do, there will be nothing up there but things I want to hide away, not children though. I let my mind stray back to that house, not because I remember the pain, but because I want to tell my mind how far I have come from those days.

It's cold but I don't mind because I have clothes that fit and match. Oh Lord those first few nights were hard. Shopping, that is what I came out for and that is what I should focus on. Oh gosh a bridge; now my dreams feel like they are forcing their way into the real world. So onwards and upwards to do the shopping, focus on the shopping girl, woman, lady or whatever.

I see the food shop and I stop to think; will it be a takeaway or a cooked meal today and how much should I buy as I am sure she will not be around again. She seems to be slipping away quite often and I wonder if she is alright or is she quietly needing some help from me and not asking.

I feel like I am very happy when I see a meal in a shop that would look like it had been cooked by me but was as easy as just putting it in the oven; oh gosh yes. A meal cooked in minutes that looks and hopefully will taste as good. When I arrive back the room looks as though it's been ransacked and whilst I was expecting, waiting almost for this to happen, it has still come as a surprise and quite a shock. She looked everywhere by the looks of things and thankfully she did not find what she wanted. Obviously, she found a bit but not the bulk of the stash and when I go to find her, I am told she has vacated her room and left. They say she left in a hurry this time and I know why.

I don't really know why I am surprised, and I remain in this state for quite some time, well long enough to burn the food. Shit, why did I leave the room and not move that stash. Thank God like I said it was not the big one, but she found it and now I am down a step. Fuck, a thousand pounds is a lot to lose when you are saving, and I really hope that she does not come back anytime soon. For one, now I have to think about securing what I have left and then find out how much Micah knows about this; that is if he knows anything at all.

I was used to Sushanna disappearing and coming back but to come back, do this and run again means something really has gone bad for her and even in my anger, I still wonder what it could be...? What would make somebody so desperate that they would just go and leave everything behind..? Oh well takeaway here I come and then maybe after eating we can figure something out.

Funny how I have not seen Micah around for a few days and my mind starts to play games with me, like have they run away together, has she harmed him and above all, does his wife have a clue about what is going on there with the two of them. I said on the day when I left that house, that nobody would ever get to use me ever again but now it seems I was a fool and that my need for somebody to lean on was my downfall. I know that I wanted to believe she was leaning on me, but the truth is that it was I who did the leaning, the needing, the longing to belong and she was just waiting for all I know to gain a moment to move on with my hard work.

A week, a month, and more passed by in a stupor with no familiar face to be seen and my back has not stopped aching. I am so not used to sleeping alone so many nights; I'm pushing cushions behind me in order to stay comfy.

Oh my f...ing word, Micah is back on the scene and has only been in the building a few minutes but he wants to talk to me about what I don't know. Maybe he wants to tell me something he can't tell his wife, poor thing. She will be hurt when she finds out the truth. I laugh to myself, but I promise myself that when

I get to his office I will keep a cool, calm, collected straight face and not judge him no matter what he says. I wonder where he will live, and I wonder what he will do about his marriage. I really hope that his wife will take this in her stride and that we will be able to remain being friends with him and me. They say God has told them to forgive so I hope they can both stick to their word and do exactly that for each other.

I take a shower and as I walk down the stairs, I notice all eyes on me and I think, 'Sushanna, what did you do?' I look at Jonah and she turns her head. Micah looks at the floor and I contain my smile, laugh quietly to myself and prepare myself to hear the tragic tale.

Micah tells me to sit, and I do so quietly whilst he hesitates and straightens his tie. He turns and half looks at me and as soon as he starts talking, he looks towards the window. "My mother has been unwell for a while. It was touch and go but she is better now and will be coming to stay with us for a bit." He continues, "She and Jonah have not really been good for each other and so I dare not take Jonah home when I need to escape the stress of being overwhelmed and then having to take care of two women." Two women I think to myself or maybe you mean three women. I choke on my laughter, but when he looks at me it is with disgust and so I turn my head. Wow this must be serious because otherwise he would have given at least the hint of a smile.

He continues to talk and as he does I realise this is not about an affair, he is not leaving Jonah for Sushanna; no this is far more serious and he does not know how to get to the point. Do I help him or I long this thing out as long as I can? Suddenly I realise I don't want to hear anymore and I want to run away, to leave the room, to hide away somewhere safe and quiet, somewhere like my room. However as he continues to talk I realise it is time for me to leave the building: Oh God, how much does he know and what does he think is going on? Do I have the courage to hear anymore or should I run now. Mentally my bags are already packed and all that remains is to find somewhere to go. He, Micah, looks at me and I look at the floor and he tells me he knows all that has been going on. Sushanna has been doing prostitution and he found this all out whilst he was away. Jonah had caught her coming out of my room with a large bundle of money and when confronted she had a massive row with Jonah. He told me that Jonah had asked her to repent, and she had said no because she had done nothing wrong. Jonah did not believe her and told her that she could have time to think it over. Sushanna ran to her room, grabbed as much as she could and ran out of the building swearing at Jonah, saying she would never return to this hovel.

Can you imagine the relief on my face? Well, how could I tell them the truth and they only told me because they knew I had been so close to her. They would not have kicked her out, they just wanted the truth, here I was knowing the truth and could not tell them. I didn't look at him, I just said I wanted to go to my room, and they allowed me to, thinking it was shock. Of course, it was shock but not in the way they thought though. It was more because it was a very close call.

I realised at that very moment that I was going to have to be more careful in my dealings and that I would now have to spend cautiously or lie to cover up why I could spend so well. Was I to say she left me money and risk them wanting to tell me to give it up as ill gotten goods; no, I'd just have to lie low for a while and be sensible.

Funny, when I was at that house, I didn't have this thing called IBS but I did now and I did not like it one little bit. I still managed to sleep, and I didn't dream about my red balloon. No, this dream was worse, so bad even I just want to forget it happened. I cry in my sleep, and I cry when I wake up. Why didn't I stand up for her, speak up on her behalf, tell them the truth or even just let them know it wasn't her. I mean it could have been anyone – but I did nothing.

The next few days went in a haze and others thought it was a matter of me being hurt by her and not the other way around. Ooh how do I make things right in God's eyes. The one good thing was I didn't have to face her. Instead, I wrote her a letter/song for if she should ever return or maybe hear it sometime or another on the radio and then I justified to myself that it was her fault for being a thief and a bad one at that.

Life returned to normal after a while and I managed to stop thinking and get on with what I had to do, back to shopping on the DL. Yes, I know slang now. Eating in my room and watching TV, a daily ritual and no more Church, well not for a while or so. I hung my cross above my bed and prayed to be forgiven, daily, hourly and even every moment that passed. That too subsided and I was able to breathe again slowly but surely. She wasn't coming back, and I was relieved. The only thing that still stung me was the money and I knew I'd have to let that go now.

Another day started and I knew I had to do something as I had been in hiding for far too long, so I got up, got dressed up and climbed out of my ivory tower. Everyone was quiet and just let me go,, to my relief. I didn't want to answer questions and they didn't want to or need to ask. They were happy to see me out and I was happy to be out.

Fernando had been discharged from the hospital and had disappeared. I didn't mind this as he had done it so often it was no longer a surprise to me: he'd be back, and we would act as though it never happened. I didn't even search for him this time as I knew that all I had to do was follow the sound of music and I would be back in his arms again. At least he didn't have to be there for all the commotion that had happened or witness the fuss that ensued. I felt quite jealous that he had been fed and watered with no effort on his behalf but nevertheless I wondered if...

15: Time – Is The Master...

Time goes quick, quicker than the blink of an eye and looking back I am glad for this. I have had the chance to settle into a kind of new normality and everyone is living their lives again and not watching me, waiting for me to fall apart. I am singing again although without Fernando and that is fine. Saved a few pennies and bought a guitar, not new but it suits me just fine. I am learning to play this thing and it is more fun than I thought it would be. Jonah plays so good and I pray one day I can be as good as she is. My stomach still hurts, and it swells so much I have to see a doctor soon and very soon. Now I am beginning to look like a balloon fit to pop any time. I wear baggy clothes because I am not sure why this is happening, and I am sure I am sick as I cannot hold food down anymore.

I still have to live though and I carry on selling for a time until my friends no longer want to see me, for whatever reason I don't know. I made sure I was careful but they don't seem to believe me anymore. So now I stop. I mean I have accumulated a lot of money so stopping for a while won't hurt will it. I have been far more careful where I stash it and I am sure I have enough for a mortgage if I want.

I am forewarned of a raid on the building so with great strategy I move the money to a very safe place and wait for all to be calm again. Of course, the police find nothing and move on as this is a Christian home, with Christians living Christian lives. Close call though – too close.

I decide that now is as good as any time to stop taking risks and so I retire from the friends with benefits game and then it happens. PAIN, oh God pain. It hurts and I can't stop it. I scream and Jonah comes running. She wants to take me to the hospital and I don't want to go but I have to. Oh God what is happening to me. What is all of this pain?

Again, pain and I cannot breathe now – oh God save me. I arrive at the hospital and I lie on the bed that moves and they rush me to a ward. Now I can't see because of the pain. Again, it hits me, and I cry out so loud all the ward can hear me. She's having a baby, I think I hear someone saying and another is telling me to push... pregnant... push... who are they talking to. No this is IBS... push... scream... pain... confusion. Now out of this confusion there is a crying and it's not me. It's a baby a girl – a baby girl and as if by magic the pain is gone. The doctors want to keep me in for a few days to make sure all is well with me after such a massive surprise and I want to stay in as I need to compute what has just happened to me. There is no doubt in my mind who the father is and after having so many friends I know for certain there was only one man who had me without protection. Fernando but I can't tell him as he has gone... somewhere.

Finally, after four days of being in bed, prodded and poked, checked and rechecked they say "You can go home" and I am pleased as there is absolutely no privacy in a hospital, on a ward with so many other mums and nurses and doctors and the list goes on... They pull the screen and as usual I hear the screams starting... another mum is about to give birth. It's funny how fast you learn but now even in the mess I recognise the voice; I should do as it held me tight so many nights. I look and I see her, she is arguing with him – my man and he is holding her hand. She is so far gone she sees no one but I am nobody's fool and I see her. *My money, My man and*

now a baby in the same hospital as me like she was spitting in my face all over again. Now she would have to pay. She would not be walking away again.

The difference between me and her is she knew she was pregnant and I didn't. She knew who the father was and she would never have told me. She knew what she wanted and after all I had been through I still never thought she would take what was mine... At least I thought he was mine. Whilst they were all concerned about her giving birth, I took a look at her records – a bit too long because they started looking for them and they would have noticed me If she hadn't screamed get this thing out of me – quite comical if you ask me. I had no time for that seeing as I was unaware of what was going on but she had the time I should have and would have had if I had known. I got her address and it was his address so I knew how to get there just not when.

Lucky for me in all the commotion they printed a new sheet and gave that to her and she was pleased. By the time she had given birth I was long gone but I asked somebody what she was having – a girl they said. It had been on her chart for the scan. I heard she planned to name the baby Sophia, my baby's name which I had told her about a long time before this. It was a name I remembered and didn't know why: or maybe it was Sophie but who cares. She was a junky and I knew that so I plotted and waited.

A few months passed and she was a few miles from me. I'd see them walking and holding hands together like I had prayed for and that stung, especially with the baby in tow. She had hurt me before but now this was the icing on the cake. Lucky for me it did not take long for her to get back into the swing of things and before you knew it, she needed a little more than him to sleep. So did he by the looks of things. She needed me and so I would be there again but not for long. She needed my arms, my hugs and she knew she could have neither. I waited until she stopped calling me and crying for me and I took her baby, my baby back. I left her a note and some money. I told her if she looked for me, I would kill her precious baby, my baby and she would always be in pain for it. He wanted to go to the police but she talked him out of it saying they were better off not being hindered by this thing. Thing you know, and now they could have fun again. I caught a bus, a train and a coach and left that life behind me again whilst running away.

Who else could have lived so much life in such a short space of time...? Now with two babies to take care of and being on the run I had to move on. I wanted to say something to Micah and Jonah, but I couldn't. They wanted my baby anyways so moving on was a must.

Money, suitcase and babies in tow I put as many miles as I could between me and them and headed towards somewhere, anywhere but where I was before. Funny how things turn out; He had kept me and now I was keeping her and nobody had fought for her or me.

Boom!!!

I'm finally a lot calmer now and per usual I did not think this thing through. I just ran. Now I have nowhere to stay, no one I can turn to and two babies in tow. Wow you are so amazingly stupid – you do not have anything in your head but air – how is this going to play out now – where are you going now.

Thought after thought attacking my mind and no answers – **STUPID FOOL**. Why did she let me go so easy and why is she not trying to find me..? Does that mean she never loved me or they just needed me – oh wow – **STUPID FOOL** – you fell for it again and now you are going to pay for this by raising their child. You can always go back and give back the girl, make them pay for what they did: you could move on and live, dance with your own child but what would happen to her, would they love her, care for her, no, they didn't even chase me for her so why would they care...?

16: Time To Move On...

It's a good thing that I know how to do certain things now and where to go to find them. People have a tendency to throw away the most amazing things and for them it is trash, but for me it is treasure. Jonah had been kind enough to buy me a pushchair and this has come in handy. A tray for carrying shopping had now been adapted, last minute style, to carry a second baby. I had baby clothes but scarcely enough for one child and my suitcase... it may be time to go back to where I started. Would he even know me anymore, and if he did remember me, would I be walking back into a trap and now not only would I be going back to a cell – so would these children.

I could kill myself or them and move on but why would you take a child only to end its life – urgh think straight. They need feeding and so do I come to think of it. I can feed me but how do I feed them? I didn't wait long enough to find out. Nappies – oh for f... sake. How, Alex, how? I always kept one piece of paper on me and when I didn't know how to read it made no sense but now I do so maybe I should take it out and read it. I remember he used to sit with me and read it and for some reason I took it from him, to taunt him, to make him pay and so that he would have something to miss.

She cries and interrupts my thoughts and so I grab her to stop her making noise and letting people know we are there. The pre–made bottles we have are running out and my boobs are so painful, it happens every time they whinge. I've seen them do this breast feeding thing and I have nothing to lose. Well not right now, so I figure I'd give it a try and as I nestle her on my chest she settles and slurps. I'll do the same for the other one when she wakes up, if I can. I may have to go back and make peace with Micah and Jonah for a while – I mean where can I go other than there. Oh God to turn up with two babies' questions will be asked. I can reduce the stress by calling ahead and telling them what has happened. Now is the time to retreat on my journey and so off I set again running in reverse. By the time I get there I am tired, really tired and I find them both talking. They opened the door like I had never left, and I am now annoyed by the fact they did not miss me.

I stiffen my back and I walk into the house like a woman now and they both give me space to pass. I give them both my hardest stare, imitating him, and I walk towards the office pushing my pushchair and heaving my case. He goes to help me but I don't need his help, so I grab it back and he allows this. I don't need them I need advice and that is the only reason I am back and as soon as I get that I will be gone again and this time there will be no reversing my decision. They know about all that happened as she had been to see them and begged for answers but there were none to give, seeing as I had gone without telling a soul. She was gone with my man but not my baby and as I had left so did she, Sushanna who used to be my love. Funny more than ever, Fernando and was supposed to be my man.

Back in my room with locks changed and babies settled, I wait for the questions to be asked and yet nobody is brave enough to raise the subject and I figure now that I am this big woman, I will do this for them. I am this child's mum, and I will raise her. I am her guardian, legal or not, I will stand by her – and now I know why I didn't have a name apart from she and her. Jonah interrupts my thoughts and to my annoyance she tells me the babies will have to be registered which I already knew, not, and Jonah knew but did not say. They will need a doctor and they need to be checked to see if they are in good health, blah, blah, blah. I want to lock her out and close the door however, the very reason I came back was for help and advice, so I decide against that idea and allow her to talk, and talk, and talk and talk. I can feel Jonah getting nervous as I grow more confident, and I am enjoying intimidating her – ooh so he did teach me well after all. Jonah makes an excuse to leave the room and I hear her say to Micah something like what happened to her, she is so cold, even becoming heartless.

Sleep was good and neither baby cried or so I believe. They look good and I think that somebody, Jonah perhaps, has had the good sense to let me sleep and deal with my girls. A knock on the door with a pattern that I knew could only be one person scares me, but I figure, face your fears and open the door. Sushanna – standing in front of me – looking me in my face – wanting to enter **My** room – wanting forgiveness. Well we all know how I think, and I warn her that entering my room may not bode well so we, meaning me, go to the lounge to talk. Funny but in all the conversation she doesn't once ask if she can see her baby or query how she might be and if she is happy. I can see it may be in her head to do this, but I don't give her the chance. I just usher her into the lounge where she sees a picture and for a few minutes she just stares at it and says nothing.

She registered Callum and told these people that she had left her with relatives to raise, naming Jonah and now fear hits me as will Jonah want to take her for real.

I don't speak but I stare, hard, and she looks at the floor whilst I look at the ceiling and all I can do is ask how I register my child. Anxious to seem helpful she tells me and so together we make an appointment to do this. After doing this I turn to her with green, cold as ice eyes, and tell her she has my permission to leave.

Without another word spoken, I rise and walk out of the lounge, and leave her looking, and hopefully feeling confused. Cold hearted has become the new word for me and now I know how he must have felt towards me and about me.

I was not his child and yet he had to look after me. Now tears are beginning to hit my face and I have to fight hard to stop them. This is not a strong woman I tell myself over and over until I get it. Why did Sushanna bother me so much and why had she become such an integral part of my life's story, almost to the point where one would think this was all about her and not me. This is about *me* and not her. This is *my story*, not hers. This is *my life*.

Sushanna died a few days later, took her own life and I did not cry, openly, but I did sing my goodbyes and henceforth I will never say that word ever again so help me God.

Amazing Grace
How sweet the sound
That saved a wretch like me
I once was lost
But now I'm found
Was blind but now I see

Ashes to ashes, dust to dust and as I walk away, I leave a massive chunk of my heart dead in that grave alongside the woman's who loved me, sometimes for me and sometimes not. I hold my head straight and my back upright, but I am still holding her hand, feeling her arms wrapped around me at night, listening to her cry and wanting to make things better for her. She was my soul and I left her to die, alone. Who had I really become and how did I get this cold and merciless. God forgive, please forgive, me.

'Twas grace that taught
My heart to fear
And grace my Fears relieved
How precious did
That grace appear
The hour I first believed

I didn't lose her because I didn't love her, no I lost her because I loved her too much

Through many dangers
Toils and snares
We have already come
'Twas grace hath brought
Us safe thus far
And grace will lead us home

See you in Heaven sis – I'll be waiting for that glorious day – one day. I will never forget you – in the meantime, in between time watch over me as I continue to live

When we've been there
Ten thousand years

Bright shining as the sun
We'll have no less days to sing I's praise
Than when we first begun

17: Me, Myself And I...

Sophie and Callum are thriving and growing fast. They both seem to look so much alike considering they both have different mums. They are my joy and hopefully I am theirs. They are registered with the same father, and I have now hidden, buried, the papers so that they don't have to see the lie that I now live. My dressing table now feels like a grave and I have to keep it along with its buried secrets. I feel like no matter where I go, I will have to take it with me to keep the secrets buried. For now, I watch the girls, my girls growing, and I feel nothing, but love and I pray I am lucky enough to keep it.

Life is returning to normality and some days I can even lock out the fears and live life like nothing bad ever happened to or around me...

The girls will need to go to school and there will be no hiding them or having them locked away. No questions about who is there or will they be found out. I laugh at them trying to crawl and falling but they laugh too, and this makes me laugh more.

They can eat, man can they eat, and I love trying to keep up with their stomachs. I try not to let others too near them, but I know I need people from time to time so I let them in but not too close, not close enough to touch them. They are here for the girls so do what you have to do and leave. Jonah tries to talk to me, but I think she knows now that I am not listening; she talks anyways, and I wait for her to finish.

When the time came for me to leave my room and move into my own home it was a shock to me even though I knew it had to happen. The girls would be one and I had to make that move. My house is so nice, and it's been decorated just fine enough to live in for the meantime, in between time. Their rooms are cute, and they are now showing signs of becoming their own people. Sophie is quiet and withdrawn at times, but Callum she is a fighter, and she will kick some ass when she is older. With their first birthday's looming, it is a rush to settle in our home and make sure they have everything they need – *so close and yet so far away*.

The house has a room at the top and in time I will lock all my secrets in there. I even go up there when the girls are sleeping and I stand by the window looking out towards the street, so beyond the view that I wished I had when I was younger. Nevertheless, the girls will not see it from here unless I am with them and even then, I will not allow the door to be closed with them in there. It gives me nightmares just thinking about it and I guess one day I will have to address that but not right now. I As I'm standing here, I can see the sea and I can see boats in the distance, I mean it's not clear, but they are there and sometimes in the silence I can hear the honk of their horns.

The house is old, and I mean old. It has big rooms and high ceilings, there are three bedrooms but the girls will share for now so there is a spare room, which maybe I can turn into a playroom for now. I can also work from that room if it suits me and keep an eye on the girls. As I paint their room, with red balloons they can reach, they sleep, and I try to keep my mind from doing over time. It seemed to work for a while but then I had to turn on the music to cut out the sounds of thinking, not too high though. If they wake up then I may as well give up for the day. I have some more furniture coming soon and the house is feeling more like a home. I didn't know of such things like online shopping and so the bidding frenzy really got out of hand.

I remember somewhere they said you should decorate the kitchen, living room, possibly dining room and bedrooms and so I have ordered a dining table, wardrobes, carpets and mats, paints and not forgetting beds. I know help was offered to me, but I will not take what I don't need from others and besides I don't want anybody dominating my home and intruding in anyway. I work hard and turn a dump into a room that I like, a lot. Now to start on my room...

Whilst I decorate, I think about working, this will have to change now that young ones are involved. I think about their father and if he would, might, just possibly want to help out a bit and then I change my mind as he had let me down to many times and allowing him in, even for an hour, might give him the impression that he can have his feet under the table. I want to say to hell with him, but I can't as words have power plus, he may think I still care.

I put blinds up at the window and although I didn't ask for this, Micah, paints my room for me. He chose a beautiful lilac for the walls and although I say nothing, I have to admit that it is rather relaxing and calm. Slowly I see he wants nothing from me and that he and his wife could actually love me for who I am and not what I give.

I relax now and cook whilst he plays with the girls, he sings, and dances and Jonah runs me a bath. Wow I could get used to this, but I watch them nonetheless. They could run off with my babies leaving me alone again and I daren't chance too much, but they don't and I feel stupid.

They have a lovely party, not that they knew any better. Cake, and juice and they tottered around looking contented, warm and loved. I don't dress them the same as they are not twins and don't have to be the same temperaments.

18: The Letter...

Throwing away old papers is an easy thing to do when you can't read but now it was a bit harder as reading everything is a fulfilment to the senses. Don't get me wrong, I have stared at this letter in its envelope a thousand times, put it away and forgotten about it but now for some reason it cannot be overlooked anymore.

I had not really noticed that there must have been a scent to it before, but I did see that there were stains like tears and I was not sure who's they were. The only thing that I could assume was they had some deep emotions in the lines written. I wondered why it bothered me now when it hadn't for years. You know what it could have even been me that stained it with the fact that each time I changed coats I put it in the pocket of the new one. The fact that I couldn't risk losing it was something, the only consistent thing of my past bought right up to the future.

Now that I have a spare moment I open the envelope again that now seems tattered and I sit down and read. Whoa, hold up, two letters are here. I'm not sure which one to read first so I look at both for a moment before deciding.

Ipsy dipsy doodle da – I'm just being childish now, I'll read this one first. Those girls put me in mama singing my own nursery rhymes too much these days.

Letter One: Part 1...

'My Dearest Enron

How are you these days. I know it's been a while and I have should have written to you sooner, but it has taken some time to summon up the courage to do this.

Look, know that when I left it hurt you but I had to go. It was hard and you know it was, but you didn't leave me much choice. I really don't want to fight with you anymore so please just hear me out.

You know that we went through some bad times but I never wanted to do what I did. I will always regret this move for the rest of my life. I saw you the other day, but I didn't see her.'

Wait, what, who...? is this about me?

'Is she still with you and if she is can I see her...?'

Confused dot com. You would be surprised the phrases you learn over time. Fudge... when you live in a Christian house you learn different ways to swear.

'I know that I ran away and left you to cope on your own, but I did try several times to come back for her and you know that I did. Let me not 'go there' as you tell me every time we talk.

I just wanted to see her, but you made that so difficult for me and that is why I did what I did. I have to have access to her, and you have no right to keep her from me.'

Holy Maloney – it was tears, I know that now.

'Do you remember when we first met, we used to talk all night about nothing and everything. Those days were so fun weren't they...? Don't tell me you don't remember because I know you do. We had no problems until she came along.'

Yup, that is definitely me. A problem to everyone. Now I'm gonna cry all over this letter.

*'You controlled everything, the finances, the house, the car and me. I couldn't breathe and so that is why I left. I wanted some space, and you knew that once I settled I would be coming back for my **Treasure – Leah**. You knew that I wouldn't leave her forever and I am begging you please, just please open the door, let me see her, talk to her, hold her – just once. I miss her so much. Does she look like me, does she still have those big green eyes, please...?*

I don't want to fight with you anymore and for the risk of repeating myself, if you don't let me have access, I will get somebody who will give me the help I need. You know I've settled, and I've met someone now who allows me to be who I am, and you know we will take care of our Treasure. I don't want to rub it in, but honesty is the best policy – and you have always reminded me of this. I don't need you to hear this news second hand. You know how much courage it takes to tell someone like you something like this. Especially as YOU don't trust ANYBODY.

Even if you would just send me a picture of her and how she looks now, I would be so happy to know that. Again please, please, please.

I did love you with all my heart, I do, did, and I promised you that. I said I do to you, and I meant it so please let me have her back and I promise I won't keep her from you.

You can see her anytime you want to, just please give her back.

Yours truly,

Your one and only Angel Autumn, now Winners'

I take a minute to breathe and then I realise I have a name. I read it two more times. Not the entire letter, just the name and I slowly come to realise it's not so bad a name. I say it in my head a few times and then I say it out loud – **Treasure – Leah.**

I don't know what to think right now and I wish I had the time to absorb all the words but time for the girls to eat and I need to tidy the kitchen. Oh crap. Crying draws me from my daydream and suddenly I am back in the real world.

"Which one is it? Cal – Cal you didn't hit Softie again did you...? You can be so spiteful for such a young child. Was she sleeping too peaceful for you, and you wanted her to wake up? You're a bit... like me and she, well she will get you back don't you fear, actually do fear." I don't mean to, but I smile at that thought.

I've learnt now to freeze food and cook it when needed so a meal doesn't take too long to put together and is on the table, under the table and in both of their hair in no time. Don't get me wrong they do eat a big chunk, but they play with it too.

Meanwhile my food is cooking, warming and whilst I wash them off, I leave it on a low heat so as not to burn.

I won't bother you with a whole day's worth of saga, but it has been full of fun, thoughtful moments and discovery.

Playtime – Story time.
Nappy change and change of clothes.
Tidy up time – Hugs time.
Bedtime television time and finally bedtime.

I would read the other letter, but I am so tired now. So, at this moment I'll just call it goodnight time...

19: A New Day

I lie in bed preparing my brain for the day and I think about what I read the night before. Would you believe it, Treasure – Leah. I was a treasure once upon a time.

I count to five and place my feet on the floor. I know the girls are either asleep or just being quiet and so I sneak to the kitchen to prepare breakfast. I knew they were up to something, and wow can kids make a mess the moment you turn your back. I am sure that ten minutes is all it takes for two girls to create chaos, and they do it so well.

The moment they settle down I ignore the mess and read:

Letter Number Two: Part 2...

'Angel'

Okay, straight to the point.

'You left us, now you can stay away. Trust, you say trust. Stay away from us and live your life. You got your man so have kids with him. You wanted freedom and you got it. Now if you come near me or her, I will kill your Treasure – TRUST ME when I tell you so.

Now you can fuck off and never come back for all I care and that is the end of it. E...

Such a short letter and I waited to read it now. I could have read that last night, maybe not, that would have kept me awake all night. It was straight to the point though!

I do notice one other thing though. There are two addresses on the first letter. Later I will look in the atlas to see where they are. One day I might even visit them who knows.

My mind wanders to buying a mobile phone. I mean I've had mobiles in the past but never new and maybe, just maybe, I will make this one a contract phone.

I stop in my tracks and think, wow. It's been a long time since I did any running, have I settled down now to a steady life – perhaps I have. I have been here a long time, for me that is, and I am actually daring to give me that chance to be happy, not for once or again, just happy. I begin to smile and then take it back. I am sure I had prayed for this once or twice, not sure, but here it is anyways. I look around to make sure nobody has seen me looking happy, then remember I'm at home so who would see?

I shrug my shoulders and head towards their room in my house, my home with laughing children, no men though, oh God, no men. I shudder at the thought, and I know I am not ready for that one yet, maybe never ever, **EVER**.

The ache for home lives in all of us
The safe place where we can go as we are
And...
Not be questioned

MAYA ANGELOU

20: Knock, Knock – Who's There...?

Another busy day has passed by and as I sit alone in the lounge, bliss. I dream of the early days I've had and the freedom I have gained. I think about the 'Voice' and wonder where he might be right now. Man, those clothes, I chuckle when I think about them, and think what I ever did with them. Did I throw them out or did I lose them along the line with my many moves? Anyway, whatever I did, they served me well.

Now is the time to settle down with a hot cup of tea, ginger biscuits and Netflix. It's not too late and Praise be, a few hours to yourself can feel like Heaven when you get them. I could have had a bath, but I feel so lazy and for once, I don't worry or stress. The bath is mine now and I don't have to fear smelling bad anymore. The public baths are now a thing of the past, and I don't have to sneak in and use their showers, pretending I was going there to swim, and now I chuckle out loud.

I'd have a glass of wine but he drank so much I am still afraid of being like him and so I decide against that. Tea is good anyways and I love the combination I've chosen.

I am watching the 'War Room,' good film and I heard them people talk about it, a lot. I decide I will check it out and I am so glad I did. It's not soppy and I need that.

– A Good Word for Such A Time As This –
hmmm.

A knock on the door jolts me and first of all I am shocked. Nobody ever knocks here, not even the postman. I look at the time and I think, too late for Jonah to knock, and so now I am curious.

In all the time I am thinking, the door knocks again and again. I wonder are they lost or just a knock at the wrong address. I know what it is, they are looking for the previous tenants, that's what it is; they'll go away once they see nobody coming but no, now they ring the doorbell. It's so loud that if they ring it once more it will disturb the girls, so now I run to beat it sounding off.

As I yank the door open, I am confronted by a pair of cowboy boots, and I know exactly who it is. I allow my eyes to slowly lift up until I see the belt. Only he wore a leather belt like that. Now I want to stop raising my head, but the momentum has already started and now must be finished. I get to his neck, his beard, his nose, his eyes, and wait a double take, he has a beard – when since did he have a beard – his eyes and now his dishevelled hair. Now that I have done toe to head, I breathe in, and I finally notice that he smells – real bad. The sympathy in me rises up for a moment then the big ugly laugh of satisfaction takes its place.

I can see he's homeless and He needs Me. What a turn around. I have stood there for what seems forever and he breaks the silence by asking to come in so now I got to make a decision. I wished he had called first but then again I may have had time to run – no it's better that it happened this way and so I step to one side and bid him pass

I make an excuse for not offering him food and drink – telling him I have nothing in the kitchen – lie, I just don't want to feed him – forgive me Father and my mind goes back to the War Room. Silently, I curse myself as I take him through to the kitchen where he can see the drinks and smell the food. Again, forever silence takes place, nobody dare speak first and we don't even look at each other. I want to speak but what do I say to him that he wouldn't expect to hear. I'm sure he is more than nervous seeing as how I treated his DLS (dirty little secret). Okay this is neither the time nor the place so we will skip this, for now.

21: The Unapologetic - Apology

I shake myself together and I look him square in the eye and now he speaks. He tells me he is sorry and that he never meant to do any of the things he did, he was stupid, and he hadn't thought about the consequences, he wishes he could turn back the hands of time and make me his again. Now I roll my eyes, and even though he see this he continues talking...

He says that he was lonely and that he needed somebody, how she was there and how she was comforting and how she was all woman, I was never like that ever with or for him. Now I look at the ceiling and press my lips together – hard.

Apparently, she cooked, cleaned, took care of him and was sexy – well what the fuck was I, sackcloth and ashes...?

He went on for what seems a year... blah, blah, blah and then *finally* he stopped. That was when I looked at him again, just to make sure he hadn't died in my house. I could see myself stabbing him but the mess, in my carpet, how about shooting him – ooh the noise. Hanging – no, too much hard work.

Instead, I asked if he needed to bathe, and he nodded. Why didn't he say no because now I would have to wash his stench out of my rug, towel and bath. I run a bath, in silence, I wash his back, in silence, I give him a towel and he dries himself off – more silence. He has something to eat and whilst he does that I put his things along with what he has used in a black bag. Then – I ask how he had found me – like I couldn't guess for myself. F...king Jonah. I know that Micah would never have told him. You see, I know that even though Micah is a Christian he is capable of being angry and hating someone and even though he can argue without shouting – I know he can when he's ready.

He asks me how his girls are, like he is really interested – sarcasm, but I tell him all the same. He seems pleased enough and so I go as far to show him a picture of them – a thing that was not afforded to or for me. He smiles and I think, 'now you can leave.' He doesn't, he doesn't even move – just sits there – staring – at the photo like he's wondering which is for who and which one looks more like him.

Now I sigh – loudly – and just as I thought, he asks which one of them is for her – now I glare – and he moves backwards abruptly. Serves him right; I can tell he is looking to stay – a place to sleep – maybe be thinks we can ignite some kind of spark, but it shows how much he doesn't know me, if he had he would have known I don't like nyam and leff (a man that someone else has slept with).

As I get up and walk towards the front door, he follows suit. I open the door and close it behind him – not before throwing his things out behind him with a sly smile. He doesn't even turn to pick it up, just walks down the path and hopefully out of my life – FOREVER.

Now back in my lounge I give him no thought and tuck back into Netflix and fun. Another movie for now... not 'The War Room.' Well, it more like watches me...

22: Freedom – Total Freedom

That is what we tell ourselves,
Until something changes the atmosphere.
Takes away our room to breathe,
Takes away the very room we came to love.

VS – ALMAC

It's been a long time since I have sung a song and I don't mean singing to the girls but singing, a real song.

I look through my CD collection, because I have one of my own now, and choose a song to dance to and sing. I want to make it a happy one, no bitterness, no hate and no disappointment, dancing and singing is the best thing for moments like that.

As I sing, I begin to clean and as soon as the girls get up they join me dancing, or in their case jumping. Pretty soon we are partying together and playing games. Most weekends I like to take them away somewhere now and today will be no exception. I pack a back pack of food, a blanket, a book for me and some drinks and after washing we are ready to go.

A quick look at the train times and we leave. One pushchair for two; Being as small as they are, I only have to pay for me and away we go. Sitting on the train I look out of the window and take in the view. I didn't do that before as I was too busy getting to and leaving somewhere, now I have the luxury of getting to rather than leaving somewhere.

Today's destination is one of my favourite places with an arcade and old pennies, an old pier and a laughing head, scared me the first time I saw it but now I use it as a landmark. A picnic on the beach and a long walk along the sea front to finish things off.

I can see the girls are growing tired now, but I make them walk a little further, that is, until Softie starts to whinge and fight to get into her carriage. Callum on the other hand looks like she could keep going a while longer and so whilst one rests the other runs.

Back home and nestled down, the girls sleep well. In fact, all night long and I love this as I clean during these times as there is no one to disrupt me or get under my feet.

I do check on them though just to make sure they are still living and breathing. I mean I am still new to this, and I don't know how life works for little babies or should I say growing babies.

23: Home

The place of safety
A place to lay your weary head,
In peace
Home – a place of warmth and
Security, hope and a brighter tomorrow.

VS – ALMAC

I have never lived alone, and I wonder how it would feel. Along the journey of my life, somebody has always been there with me and even though I have the girls, I still consider this as being alone – not lonely but just alone.

Another day over and I snuggle down again to dream.

A knock on the door – what now – a pattern and I suddenly know who it is.

I run to the door and open it quick and there he is again. This time I don't want him here. He smells again and I know he wants what he got before. This time I am a bit more unwilling for him to stay and as soon as he has done what he needs to do, I kick him out and throw out his things as usual. I may have to buy spare towels now so as not to lose a lot of things that I can't afford to lose.

Now I'm worried about what is coming, still I got rid of him faster tonight and no sign of him asking for the girls.

A few nights go by before he visits again, and I did try to hide but his persistent knocking drives me mad and so I let him in. This time he stays in the spare room as times are getting colder. When we wake up, he has his breakfast in his room as I want to keep him away from my girls. He can hear the girls laughing and playing but he doesn't come out of the room to see them.

His visits are becoming more and more frequent, and I am not sure I like this – bloody – Jonah, I know she let him know where I was and now, I may never get rid of him. He wants to stay but I tell him that the girls need to start a nursery and I have to see about getting them into a good one. I know he's lazy and doesn't want to do hard work, so he agrees to go. Not sure how long I can keep this going. It's like I now live a double life in my own home.

That night – I sit agitated and waiting but he doesn't turn up and I sleep with one eye open – just in case he may knock, and I want to be ready for this – anything could happen.

I wake the girls and I am so tired I just want to go back to my bed. He, Fernando, has really started to mess up my life and I think about leaving, but no this is *my home*, *my girls*, *and my life*.

Speak of the devil and he is sure to appear. He is at my door again and again. He enters in and I make him, or should I say, warm his food and he eats; not like the hungry eating but the kind of comfortable, feet under the table eating.

I don't know what to do now and suddenly in a moment of what I call weakness he kisses me. I don't respond at first, but then

I do – just for a moment before remembering all that he did, and I pull away. I forgot how tender he felt, how sweet he could look and how much I loved it when he touched me and held me with those strong arms.

He stays in my room, and we sleep well. We've made love and I am not sure where this will lead but for now it feels really good. This was happening so fast or way too fast, who knows.

Letters plunk through my door and I go to pick them up. I'm only gone but a moment but by the time I've made the tea he is up and getting ready to leave. Well, the least he could have done is drink the tea, seeing as I've made it, but he has no time and has to go. He asks if I'm going anywhere, and I reply no hoping that he won't be long. Funny how we fall so fast for things that are no good for us, but I know, knew, him and I was in no hurry to get to know something new.

That night right on time he was back, and dinner had been cooked, girls in bed and another kiss waiting. Sex waiting too and I am not going to lie, I thought I was over that but obviously not.

The girls came racing into my room seeing as I had overslept and were taken aback by the fact that mummy wasn't alone.

I don't know how he does it but one smile from him and the charm had begun. Before long he had them jumping on the bed, laughing and enjoying him as much as I was.

How much better could life be with the girls in nursery, a man in my life, a new job in the making and I even dared to think well maybe if a marriage like Micah and Jonah, was on the cards.

The job was good but hard and it was a good thing that he was around to take the girls to and from school, although we didn't explain to him them who he was and how he was connected to them.

Life became a normal thing and yes, he did disappear a few times but never that long and he always bought gifts back for us. I didn't worry as I got help elsewhere when he wasn't around. I mean what could he do in such a short space of time. I mean everybody needs a breather from each other and we have just gotten back together anyhow.

24: Viola Still Lives

I guess with all the things that were happening and changing in my life, I should have stopped and taken a better look at what was happening and things that I should have seen I didn't. To be honest they were so small to me that I perhaps overlooked them or maybe just didn't take the time to understand or acknowledge them the way I should have.

I was working and he had become a stable part of my daily living to the extent that he even became a steady part of my daily existence.

I didn't take the girls out as often anymore because he didn't like me being away so much and I accepted that, so far as to ask permission each time we did go out. He liked to bring a few friends around the house, and I made sure they were taken care of even though I didn't join in with the conversation, until I was called to serve and then I would give my small but simple commentaries.

I did feel used at times but doesn't everybody and so I locked that away in the back of my head. I noticed that the girls would become quiet on his entry into the house, but they were growing up and sometimes kids just need their space and quiet. They stuck with each more these days and rarely came downstairs. Now that they were a bit bigger and more capable of tidying behind themselves, it seemed only fair for them to have their own rooms and so this was given to them. I did notice that they stayed together but to be fair it had been that way at the start and so changing this was going to take a bit of time – I supposed.

Other than that, things were moving along nicely as they should. Fernando now had a key and was moving in on a permanent basis and to my surprise he settled well. The girls needed adjusting they got used to seeing him in my bed, our bed.

Life was truly amazing, and I was blinded with happiness. Meals made and house cleaned, I gazed at the clock that had been newly put up and felt satisfied with the day's work.

I had in essence become all the things that I guess most women might have wanted out of life and some of them might have been jealous even of what we had. That was their business though, I didn't care, let them keep wishing as what I wanted all day long I had and a bit more.

We had our arguments from time to time but nothing to write home about. All barring nosy Jonah telling me that perhaps I, after she had shown this man where I was living, had rushed into this too fast. I knew what I wanted and in my eyes she was way too contrary for my liking. I let her talk some days but on other days, I had no time to listen to her twaddle so whilst she talked, I cleaned or did what I had to do. One day I even walked out of the house with her talking. I had gotten so used to the background noise she had become like the television; apart from the fact you couldn't switch her off. I laughed when I thought about that day, but she didn't. She will or would one day.

I think that was the first time it ever happened, and I was so confused. He had been out all day and when he had come home, he was tired, he had a headache, and I was excited about something or another. He told me he knew that Jonah had been round that she was no longer welcome. This was confusing as he knew he was my man now and nothing that she said changed anything.

I was, as it's called, blindsided and no I didn't see it coming. I felt it a few seconds later to show how much I didn't expect it. He made it clear after that she was not to come back and so I nodded as speech was definitely not happening. After he left the room, I cleaned my face. I mean there were no tears as though the shock of it all didn't allow me to think for tears.

Jonah did visit but now in secret and certainly not when the girls were around. Barring that we were fine. If we argued I made sure Cal – Cal and Softie were nowhere in sight or in earshot and I would try to keep it as quiet by not shouting back or igniting a bigger flame than needs be. If he came home quietly, I would hide in the girls' room and only come out when he had fallen asleep. I would read them a story or clean so that if he approached their room, he would not become suspicious of anything. If he came home singing, I knew all was well with him, but I dare not sing with him unless invited to do so. This meant I was included.

It's so easy to change the mood of a man by saying silly things or even doing silly things and so I try my hardest not to. I even make mental notes to myself like; try harder in future, or remember not to say that again, go there or behave like that. I mean we are learning each day how to be a couple, and this is not always easy is it...?

I got started with the loft and making it a room and not just a loft. It had stored so much rubbish just dumped there, and I quite happily cleared it all out. I still didn't want the girls up there and so I locked it whenever they were up or playing hide and seek.

25: Viola Takes Over

I got up as usual and tottered around the houses before whisking Cal-Cal and her sister off to school. Gotten on my brand-new motorbike and rushed off to work. Another birthday coming up and I love a good celebration. I decide to stop at the shops on the way home to buy some small gifts – now whilst shopping I see some really nice things and I am buying them.

I approach the till and I am so confident. Smiling I put the things to be paid for but it rejects my card – how did that happen when I had three hundred pounds on the card. I try again and again it rejects my card. I have no choice but to call Jonah and despite all that he has told me, I also don't want him to think I have been frivolous with my, our money again. She meets me and agrees to pay for the goods, and me paying her back when I have it on payday. We reach my, our, home and unpack. I did not know he would be home earlier than usual, and he sees her there.

He greets her warmly, looks at me and makes and excuse; tired, long day etc and leaves the room. The party is so nice and relaxed – a few friends round and cake along with drinks all devoured the cleaning begins. Party games being run by Jonah whilst I pack bags and with all the children gone, I sit down to relax before making dinner.

He makes me jump coming into the room the way he does, and I don't know how to judge his mood as he is smiling but his eyes look stern. I don't know whether to run or hug him. Fernando stands in the doorway as I try to leave, and I sense now he is not happy. I tell him his food is on the fire and it will burn; he is oblivious to my words and does not move – not an inch. He just smiles and looks at me, then he kisses me, and I am slightly but not totally nervous. I find a space and squeeze through.

In the kitchen I breathe in and hold it for a second too long because as I turn around, I am hit. The chair I had forgotten to return to its place comes hurtling towards me and without a second thought I raise my hand to defend myself. Man, it hurt and this time I scream, loud. On hearing this, my girls come running and are stopped by Fernando blocking the doorway. He does move fast. They are scared now but he explains that I have fallen and that he will help me up, no need to be concerned. They both look past him at me for confirmation and although I am crying, I nod in agreement. To go against him I guessed at the moment was not going to make the situation better I try to keep the crying quiet although the pain is so bad, I can't bear it.

He takes me to the hospital, and I am seen to. He is a charmer, and the nurses are enamoured with his words – they look at me harshly and I can tell that they wish they had him as their man. Handsome, cool looking and clear skin; well he was my man and nobody, but I could love him the way he needed to be loved.

Back home and I realise my mistake, I had left the girls by themselves. They are crying and scared and as soon as we enter the house they run to me like frightened kittens. Soon they are purring and holding me tight. I made a mistake, one that I am not sure of, but it must have been my mistake as he would never do anything like this without a justifiable cause, would he...?

He doesn't talk to me he just leaves the house slamming the door and I daren't call him back or question anything, not at this moment in time.

When he does come back, he lets himself in and brings a bottle of wine up to our room. We drink and laugh and then make love, all night and despite the pain I am glad he is happy with me now.

This is certainly not idyllic but nevertheless in order to survive we all have to find a strategy. This is my way I guess and so far it has worked. Remember, I was a seller and it worked with weary husbands and bullies alike. Now I formulate a plan for it to work on him. Come think to of it, did I save some bad marriages when some sad neglected wife had now gotten themselves a more relaxed and responsive husband.

Guilt works well for a while but not forever and it is not long before his moods are changing toward me once more. I daren't say anything as it is not unexpected for Viola to enter the room or for me to suffer the consequences of a word spoken out of line. Now I have learnt to cry in silence and sometimes when I am not careful, I see the girls giving me looks like they are scared for me.

I get angry with them for this and shoo them out of my room. Softie cries way too easily and I have to tell her mummy is tired, mummy just needs space, mummy didn't mean it. Cal-Cal on the other hand gives menacing glares before steering her sister away from the door and back into their haven I think if she could spit on me she would. I hazard a guess at where she may have picked this behaviour up from and I say it must have been me; I am used to blaming me for everything.

He has gone again and during this time I take time to pull myself, my life and all that I know back to normality. My money has gone down again and this time I know it can't be me and so I phone the bank to argue about why they are stealing from me.

Now I find out that the man I love, loved, love has been taking it. I had given him my pin and he was spending whilst I worked. Now I change the pin and pray to God that he doesn't realise that I have found out about the second card that he has forged. I think he doesn't as I have not been beaten and so for now, I am safe – ish.

26: Viola – Why Won't You Leave Me ALONE?

The sum of all knowledge you have
Over someone
Is the sum of power you have
Over that same person

VS – ALMAC

I am still trying to be normal but now I hide my card and have opened a second account to which I can move spare money to. One needs to be prudent these days. He comes home and asks for money openly now and I have to say I have none to give. He knows I am lying but he can't tell me how he has been living off me and so does not reply. He wants my card, but I say there's been a problem with it and the bank want me to contact them. This works and he shuts up as he is unaware that I already know.

He leaves for a few days but not reminding me he needs money. I sink into the chair behind me and think hard about how to escape this one.

Contrary to the way some people think, they do not know just how hard it is getting part pay and part benefits. It's not an easy thing and surviving off that small amount of money is even harder with some man demanding the little bit that you do get. Let's face it, he knew how much I got and sometimes I'd hide a bit here and there, but he didn't care enough to fight me all the time.

I would do odd jobs here and there like cleaning for the rich Jewish woman down the road and I would add things to her shopping list, when I thought she hadn't noticed, to take home to feed my girls. When she found out I begged her for forgiveness, and she barely forgave me for my erroneous behaviour but told me in future to be honest. I did feel guilty and when she found out I had to profess my wrong doings; it was hard. I had starved and I didn't want the same thing for my girls, who does...?

I could see the girls were a bit, just a bit (sarcasm), afraid of him too and this was one thing I hated even more than what he was doing to me. The moment he came through the front door, the girls would run to me and hold me tight. They weren't supposed to know that kind of fear. I had promised them that and now the promise had been broken – by a man.

Now something has to be done and so quietly I pack his things and I move them outside for him to collect, locks changed and fear sinking in for what is ahead I wait. I wait and I wait – months go by, and I still wait. I'm hesitant when I go out. I am hesitant when I go to work, fearing what I will find when I get home and I am even more fearful about leaving the girls at school. Nobody, not even them has been told the truth, but at least the clothes have gone; I know he has collected them.

A few more months go by before I get a call to say a window has been smashed and yes, I know what it is.

I arrive home and quietly, steadily and he is sitting on my bed, glaring at me. Asks me if I thought he was a fool, did I think I could get away with this shite and what would happen to me if I dared to be so stupid again in future. He demands my keys and I hand them over. He has told the neighbours he got locked out, lost his keys and that explains the broken window.

He tells me that the next time I dare to do this he will go to Social Services and tell them about me and what I had done to Sushanna.

Little does he know; I have been living a double life by now. Well, when you are going through this kind of thing you need a little tenderness too and I needed it.

This man has no name and never will because I do not love him. I just need to feel better about myself, and he does that for me. I can say I have never had sex like this before and I am enjoying it. I once tried to take him home, but fear overtook me, and I diverted him to my old dumping ground. All of this during the day with the girls at school and me supposedly at work.

It's not long before I find out I am preggers and not sure who the father is. I ingest some serious alcohol and hope to lose it but no such luck for me. I have to tell him, and I am not surprised by the fact that he tries to kick my baby out of me. For this, he is given a suspended sentence. Can you believe it? This is his first crime, and he has witnesses to say generally he is a good man, a charming man, a well-spoken man, a kind-hearted man who would do anything for anybody.

I cry all the way home with him beside me laughing at me all the way home. How could they believe him? A further court hearing is set but I do not turn up because it would do no good anyway and he comes home as free as a bird.
I have got no one to turn to – at the least no one I can trust.

I lie in my bed, and I listen to a song I haven't heard in a while and as the song plays, my brain digests the words, they are then conveyed to my heart and my heart breaks. It is shattered into a million pieces as I realise this is my life and there is no escaping it...

Because of depression, I have been let go from my job and my other man is on hold – for now. I have no time for thinking as I have to appear normal to the outside world as well as to my girls. My stomach is growing and this time I know for sure. However, I am not sure how this will pan out, so I act, for now, as though I am on a boat heading down a river in Egypt.

When I started seeing him, it was a bad day, and I had no intentions of falling in love but I did and for some reason fall in need of comfort. I never expected for it to go this far, and I almost certainly had no intentions in telling the world he existed. He was my, for the want of a different word, secret. My safe place, someone who I could hide away with and as ashamed as I am, he was my safety net; not even to catch me when I fall, just to hide me until I could lick my wounds better, to regather my train of thoughts. Now there was the risk that somebody could find out and cut a gaping hole in my net.

I had to question myself again as to whether I was even in love with him, and the answer was emphatically no – same as before. I do this from time to time. I ask the same question like the answer will change but we all know it won't. It's always the same with Fernando – **do you love me – yes** – do you love me – yes – and yet one of us is lying – and that will never change – well for now anyways.

27 The Journey Begins

Naivety is a gift granted
To those who do not grow
Cannot grow due to lack of education or
Refuse to grow either – SPIRITUALLY or MENTALLY
Do not be that person – always strive to grow

VS – ALMAC

More months go by in a haze and my ever-growing stomach is only saved by the fact that the girls are excited about my baby. They have saved her life.

We lie and tell the world that he is the father, and it is to be kept that way; any deviations from this and I am sure to lose her for good. I can't afford for this to happen and so I keep the pretence of being happy and of having a loving partner.

He wants to marry me and have his name added to the tenancy. Anybody who knows him as well as I do would know this is just another step toward controlling me. I tell him that for now let's just go ahead with the housing situation and leave the wedding until my baby is born. I mean I don't want to walk down the aisle with a big stomach – it wouldn't look good and so now I only have a few months to get it all done and I have to think fast.

I may have been naive when I left that house, but she is no longer me and I am no longer her.

SHE IS DEAD TO ME NOW – NO LONGER TO RISE EVER AGAIN

Writing little notes to myself, to remind me of who I am, has really helped me to survive these days and I read them repetitively like a lost person hoping and praying to be found. Finally, I give up, get up and get dressed – time for action.

I make a list of what has to be done and I call Micah. I have to call a few times because that stupid Jonah keeps answering the phone and just as I think of giving up an angry Micah answers the phone. He is demanding to know who is calling and hanging up, why are you calling and not saying anything. I take a deep breath and go for it, telling him everything – even things I had not dared to tell anyone before. I hear the occasional okays and yeses and then without even saying a farewell the phone goes dead. I had begged him not to say anything to Jonah but whether he has listened to me or anything I've said is anybody's guess.

I sit in silence just looking at the walls – oh God what did I just do...? Pain attacks me and I can't move – fear – like I have never experienced in a long time grips me and I cry out.

It isn't long before the door knocks, and I am rooted to the spot out of fear. Opening the door could be the worst thing I do right now. The door keeps knocking and when I get there I am relieved to see Micah standing there – alone.

He has papers in his hands for me to sign and I read them becoming more and more able to deal with what is going on inside my head. Without speaking I take the pen and sign the form and now I know things will be alright. Well in this certain case it will be. Micah is angry and I know he is angry with me, but him holding it back right now is what I need. In minutes he is gone, and I am alone.

I go to the council as arranged and bring the papers back saying he is on the house now. Funny that, I had no need to worry because he never asked to see proof. He must have realised I was too fearful of him to lie

I guess now that he knows he has full control of me, the girls and even the baby he leaves the house full of overt confidence. He does not come back for months at a time and during this time I give birth to my girl – Angel-Neveah, born on a Friday 8th June and so full of fire. I really love her, but I am scared for her too. She didn't ask for this and I am sure she doesn't deserve any of this either.

Every time he returns to my home, the house or should I say this dwelling I try to keep her out of his way and in her room. This is not easy as she cries all the bloody time; she in not like the other two, she is a lot of hard work, and she tires me easily. I mean it's not like I don't love her, I do, but sometimes, just sometimes...

He turns up and eats food, even if there isn't enough, he eats and then he watches the television. Dare I say anything, and the violence starts? I swear sometimes all I have to do is sneeze and he is ready to beat me and then tell me it's all my fault. The girls when hearing this are now running scared all the time and a lot of the times they leave the house with the baby in tow – heading to Micah and Jonah's.

Cal-Cal, is always the one to ask mummy to come with them and Softie is the one to lead the run whilst Cal-Cal grabs her sister Angel. Neither of them know how to take care of a baby and soon we have Jonah on our case – she is telling me to give her the kids for a while, just until I sort myself out and I let her take them. I cry a lot and some more and then I return home to cook like nothing has happened. As I cook, I mourn the leaving of my girls at somebody else's home, like strangers and not mine, like I didn't care but I did, I did, I really do love them.

Jonah was like a punch in the face, telling me how well they were all doing and how happy *MY BABIES* were – *MY BABIES*. You would have thought she had given birth to them, and she rubbed it in like salt in a wound and how much they were learning. Well, you didn't do that I did all of that. *I DID THAT NOT YOU*.

28: The Loft

A few days turned into a few weeks and then eventually a month turned into two, then three and before you knew it Christmas was on its way. I just knew I had to take my girls back.

Having them back in the house was one of the weirdest feelings ever and I knew it would take time for them to settle in again. I was willing to try, if not for me, for them.

We lived quietly for almost another six months and in that time my last daughter would be not too far from one. We were going to have the best time ever and I was going to cook up a storm of food now that I knew what to do and how to love them. Angel was so quiet now – not a sound from her. She even looked lost, and I wondered if I had lost her forever, but I had no time to focus fully on that.

Whenever she did cry, she would look at Callum, as if to say, come for me, rescue me, love me and Cal-Cal would. She'd come running and baby girl would smile, stretch her arms up and be warmly held. Callum had always been strong but now I could see just how strong she really was.

She was big sis in one aspect but also mum in another and whilst I praised her openly for this, I was secretly jealous. Callum was a baby and yet she was still more like a mother than I was. My Angel did not love me and nor did she want me near her. I couldn't hold her without her crying and as for trying to hug her; it was like hugging an ice block. She just wouldn't let me, and I didn't know what I was doing wrong.

Night after night alone in my bed I cried. I cried for me, cried for the future I had always dreamt of and knew now it would never be mine. I cried for my girls and as I drank myself into oblivion I cried for any reason whatsoever. Believe me when I tell you I even cried for Fernando. Each day I rose and carried on as best as I could, taking them to school and returning home to sleep – no cooking – no singing – no dancing and no joy.

I lost all track of time during this time, and it all became like a hamster going round on a wheel. I did all the things I should, at the right times, with a big smile and I prayed that no one and nobody saw through my guise. Maybe they did but I was so drunk I didn't see it and maybe I was so locked in my own prison that I stopped caring what others thought of me anymore.

I was a shell of me, and I knew it. For the first time ever I had become all that I had hated about him.

Christmas came and went in a haze. Angel's birthday did the same thing and all the while I was a spectator in my own life. He came and left when he felt like it and we lived a life like hater and hated. I never knew now when he would turn up and to be quite frank, it didn't matter.

Every time he was there it was beatings and arguing, the girls hiding and all of us scared out of our wits. Sometimes I would wonder if the neighbours were hearing any of these incidents as they said nothing to us and turned their heads when we left the house. Some days were so bad that things would go flying out of the window and I wondered when it would be my turn or even one of the girls. I knew it would be more likely to be

Angel as he knew she was not his. She was cold too and stared at me with eyes as cold as ice. She spat at me and even tried to hit me – just like daddy did.

She was only a baby, and this is what she was doing already. Only Cal-Cal knew how to make her calm down and I felt too much responsibility was going on such a young child and so I agreed to send her back to Jonah, just for a while. I told myself – 'just for a while.' My baby was leaving me again and this time I knew she was never coming back.

In the middle of the night I was woken up by a sharp slap and as I opened my eyes another slap came my way. Slap after slap and shouting. I could not think, no time to think – what was happening.

Fernando had been seeing someone else and she was pregnant – for him. Now it was time for him to move me out of my home, but he couldn't as his name was not on the tenancy rights. He slapped me harder and harder. I couldn't move or do anything but take it. The girls were screaming and so was I, but I took the beatings.

It was not until he grabbed the girls and told me that I would never see them again that I did what was right. I got the courage to stand to my feet and run towards him. I was begging him to give them back. I had already given up my baby and now he wanted to take them too – no – that was too much.

I knew I had something in my hand when I hit him the first, the second, the third and the fourth time. Now there was so much blood I didn't know which blood was his and which was mine.

Instead of stopping to think, I grabbed the girls and headed for the front door but he blocked me and so I headed for the loft.

We locked ourselves in the loft and I left the key in the door to stop him from getting in. I sang in my head at the beginning and then sang out loud to the girls. I could hear him smashing the house to bits. I could only imagine how much of my hard work he had destroyed but I didn't care. I was terrified of the loft but for the first time I felt safe, and I was not coming out.

At some point I must have fallen asleep and given the fact that the girls were in shock they left me alone. We were hungry but we stayed put. We even peed in bottles so as not to leave and even when they cried I made them stay right where they were.

29: The spoken Grief

I have loved you and I have hated you.
I have wanted you and I have wanted to let you go.
I have discovered a dream and I have discovered a
nightmare.
But I have never discovered me.

I have seen the wonders of the world,
And all the truth flung far wide and unfurled.
I have been through desert places that eyes should never
see,
But now I just want to break free.

I have heard his story and her story, but my story is me.
I have granted wishes but my wishes.
I need to be accepting my wish to grant me the longing of
love,
So, bye history you are in the past for me.

If you don't know which way you are going history
How the heck do you expect me to.
If you don't know what you want out of life history
How the heck can I give it to you.
Either you stand history, or you sit
You either give history or take history.

But you better make up your mind,
Because history you have run so much
That you are running out of time.

Don't touch me don't come near me, get out of my dreams.

Don't look at me, oh don't you dare look at me,
And I won't look at you.
No, not today and not tomorrow.
Cos this time history we are through.

If history is repetitive... Break the cycle

VS – ALMAC

30: The Aftermath

Coming out of that room for the first time was scary and I wasn't sure if he would still be there waiting to continue what he had started but as I gingerly went toward the stairs, I could tell he had gone.

My house was a mess, and I didn't care. I grabbed the girls and headed to Micah's. My face said it all for him and he was so helpful to us.

Kettle on and girls in another room to play, only Callum wanted to keep checking on me; she was way too old for her age and so each time she came back I smiled. Despite my face aching – I smiled, despite being in pain – I smiled, and despite wishing I were dead – I smiled.

I had cracked ribs; a blackened eye and my beautiful lips were fuller but – I smiled.

I was told I could take him to court, and they would make him pay this time but I remembered the last time and refused. I was not being put to shame again – no way was that ever going to happen, not to me and this time I meant it.

Oh, they begged, pleaded even and tried to do bargains with me – even told me how brave I had been that night. Truth be told I didn't hit because I was brave – I had hit him because I was scared, not just for me but for the girls and I knew if I didn't do something, he would have killed us all.

He was no longer our problem. He was hers and *I didn't care...*

31: Another Journey

Sometimes, the only way to face your future is –
To confront your past
I do not mean retreat to your past – I mean
If the past has overwhelmed your present
Face it, overcome it and then you will be able to learn
how to leave it where it is – In The Past

With babysitter sorted, reassurances given *TO SELF* and map in hand, I headed out on my journey to where it all began – or so I believe it to be.

I have to be honest, with every step I take I am increasingly aware of the fact I now need the toilet. I am not good with facing things, I am not a fighter, and I am easily overcome by situations out of my hands. In essence I am a coward – changing this will be a hard thing to do but nevertheless it will have to be done.

Bus routes checked, double checked and rechecked; I board and take a seat. Looking out of the window at the view decreases the stress although it does not totally eliminate them completely.

My logic does not seem logical, but it works for me as I have memorised the stop before the one I need to get off at. This way I can prepare myself to stand to my feet and gain at least a modicum of bravery to get off the bus.

This, would you believe, is just the first leg of the journey. Now I am to board a train and with a pre-bought ticket in hand I board my train. This bit seems longer than it actually is but at least it has given me time to release some thoughts.

The stop that I need is close to the address I need so I get off the stop before so that I can walk off some fear.

Address Number 1:

Turning the corner, I start to remember; I can see an image of me running scared, no shoes, no coat and no direction. I step to one side as though I am watching that person running past me. I turn as though to watch her run and wonder why she hadn't seen the station that I had seen, right there. It's only then that I realise I am being watched – watching some invisible person and I laugh. I laugh partly because I feel stupid, partly because I remember I escaped and partly because looking back now I can see how funny I must have looked to others who didn't understand.

Now I can move onwards and with map in hand again and again I check the address. Here it is and today the house looks much smaller than I remember. I approach the door and knock very quietly like I don't really want anyone residing inside to hear. To my disgust and fear I hear footsteps towards the door, and I step back to prepare myself for what may be inside.

The door opens sharply, and I almost jump out of my skin as I step back, at this hand of a giant, I exaggerate, man grabs me and me being who I am pull away and fall, flat on my gluteus maximus – "you backside" he says and I laugh – did he just make a joke. As I have laughed, he does too and now when the hand reaches out to me I take it, I stand and wipe myself down. I think he only invites me in because I am hurt, and he leads me to a big room where I can sit and recover. Now I can see I don't remember anything about this house anymore. It's brighter, smells nice – very nice and there is a smell of food – nice food – coming from somewhere.

"Andrew" he says as I enter, "Sit down." "Angel" I say in return.

As we conversate, I know it's not a word – he must guess I used to live – if you can use that word – in that house. He asks me if I would like to look around and for want of a better phrase, I say, "fuck yes."

As he shows me around I think dang this house has so many rooms and yet I only ever had access to one. I ask what happened to the old man who lived there before, and he tells me his dad – fuck – his dad has now been moved to the old folk's home round the corner. I ask where to, carefully avoiding going near there, he doesn't even know me, but he tells me anyways. Now before I can think we are approaching the dreaded room and my heart lurches. He is oblivious to my plight and throws open the door. For a moment I think I will be thrown inside and the door locked – call it over imagination.

It's beautiful and it is bigger than I remember; the window is open, and it is painted white. He recalls it being dingy and so do I – to myself. He says he didn't like this room back in the day and so to overcome the feeling he painted it as bright as he could, and I know how he feels but I say nothing. He uses it as a library and sits in there to play his music seeing as how he found some old CD's up there.

He says it's his favourite room – not mine.
He says it brings him joy – not me.
He says he likes to sleep up there – hmmm, not if he knew what I knew.

He says it has a beautiful view – I take a look and all of a sudden I don't feel as bad as I did before.

I thank him for the tour, and he invites me to visit again. As I say yes, I think maybe I will tell him who I am and how I know the house, suddenly I see a picture – of me; now I guess he already knows who I am. I tell him my name – again and he tells me his – Andrew, again. Now I think I will go back one day with my girls.

Address Number 2:

Again, a little bit of a walk, no bus to get to this address and I stand across the road for a while staring across the road at a smaller humbler house. I'm surprised at how close it is to the first place.

I cross the road nervously and I approach the door and hear happy laughter coming from within but before I have the chance to knock a young man and woman open the door. Fear grips my chest so bad I run back across the road.

As I look over my shoulder an older woman comes out to say bye. I allow myself to look at her and then continue running. I am sure she sees me as I run away. I am not ready to be seen yet.

What if she rejects me...?

Is it her in the first place...?

How can somebody who doesn't even know you reject you...?

Why didn't I give myself the chance to see if I even look like her...?

Is she even old enough to be my mum...?

Who knows but for now it will have to wait. I am hungry and I need a place to rest. I walk for a while and I find a Travelodge, again. I laugh as I remember the voice and I wonder if I will perhaps bump into him. 'Don't be so stupid,' I rebuff and walk inside to book a room and not behind the building to beg food.

Now I realise how far I have come from those days.

Sleep is amazing and the food so nice and warming. I now make a phone call to let everyone know I am alright and that things are going well and hearing a sigh of relief down the phone makes me feel better – somebody cares – somebody **really** cares.

The next day I am supposed to leave but I ask if I can book one more night – seeing as I can – smirk. They have to move me to another room and seeing as they do that, I book for three nights more.

Now I can look around the area I never knew, and I can relax before going back.

I stay around the hotel for the day and now I see the river, the trees and the park. Wow, why didn't I see any of this before and why do I only remember it being dark and dirty. I find a pier and I walk along it. There's a train that runs along it and I am told this pier is a mile long.

I walk down it, turn back and walk back. Now hungry I head back to the hotel and eat, go back to my room and relax watching television and read a book – because I can...

When my door knocks, I jump up and hide. 'You are so stupid' I tell myself, then I'm angry because somebody should have known better than to knock like that and scare me. I shout out "what do you want?" and am surprised by my own aggression, but I like it.

I head back to the house and this time I am bold enough to knock the door. A little lady opens the door and in my eyes, she looks like me. This time I ask for the first address hoping it will spur some kind of memory but I guess it doesn't as she gives me directions and so I leave, but before I do, she asks if she knows me. I say "no" and walk away. Maybe one day but not today.

With my hotel stay over I go home to start again but this time afresh and happy. Past behind me, new beginnings in front of me and exciting new things to try... because now it really *IS MY LIFE.*

Printed in Dunstable, United Kingdom